OTHER WORKS BY CRAIG TERLSON

NOVELS

CORRECTION LINE

FALL IN ONE DAY

SAMURAI BLUEGRASS

SHORT STORY COLLECTION

ETHICAL ASPECTS OF ANIMAL HUSBANDRY

NOVELLA

BENT HIGHWAY

LUKE FISCHER

SURF CITY ACID DROP

MANISTIQUE

THREE MINUTE HERO

PLAYS

ACK NOW

PRAISE FOR SURF CITY ACID DROP

"An absolutely fantastic read that has you rooting for Fischer from the start. The perfect blend of Pacficos, peanuts, and knees to the balls."
- *Andrew Geisbrecht (CAN)*

"There's plenty of humour, many opinions on coffee, beer and breakfast options, as well as some absolutely kicking fight scenes... This was one road trip that had me absolutely tripping. Great stuff."
- *Lagoon (UK)*

"An exhilarating read with memorable characters and high action excitement. Buy the book, take the ride."
- *S.L. Keenan (UK)*

"God I love detective stories set in hot places... There's something that heady mix of violence, danger, clever quips and tropical sunsets that just spells out perfect escapism for me. Definitely worth reading."
- *Amy Gagnon (CAN)*

"A crime novel filled with good food, good drink, and punches to the head. The character Mostly Harold takes over any scene he is in and takes us all on a menacing and often hilarious road trip from border to border."
- *Kenneth M. Gray (USA)*

PRAISE FOR MANISTIQUE

"Terlson creates an atmosphere I cannot get out of my head. The characters made me laugh, they made me ponder life mysteries. Great action, great dialogue."
- *Scott M. Frederick (USA)*

"What a phenomenal book Manistque is... A masterclass in crime fiction."
- *Steve Griffths, author of Kill Sequence (UK)*

"There's plenty of slam-bang action in this story, and a good dose of surprising twists and turns. Highly recommend for fans of noir crime drama with unforgettable characters."
- *Douglas W Lumsden, author of the Alexander Southerland P.I. books (USA)*

"Well-written crime story from a real talent. Terlson deserves to be a household name with a wide readership."
- *Jeff Bartholomew Stevens (USA)*

PRAISE FOR SAMURAI BLUEGRASS

"Pitch-perfect and haunting. Five stars."
- *Ed Church, author of the Brook Deelman mysteries (UK)*

"A classic stranger in a strange land tale that Terlson riffs on and makes it wholly his own. Bluegrass is chock full of compelling characters, mysterious happenings, transmigrations and absolutely breathtaking turns of phrase."
- *Anthony Perconti (USA)*

"Wildly inventive and entertaining novel—absolutely recommend!"
- *Thomas Trang (UK)*

"The parallels of mastering the stroke, with a brush or sword, were breathtaking storytelling techniques."
- *Margie Peterson (Reedsy Discover)*

"Loved this book! Drew me in immediately. Do yourself a favour and pick this up and/or any other wonderful novels by Craig Terlson. You won't be disappointed."
- *Offer Kuban, Host: The Speakeasy Podcast (CAN)*

PRAISE FOR THREE MINUTE HERO

"Best yet in the Luke Fischer oeuvre."
- *Linda Robinson (USA)*

"First-rate modern noir."
- *Carol Reid (CAN)*

"A fast-paced engaging story with great dialogue … Read it, you won't be disappointed."
- *Linda KS (USA)*

"This book is like a road movie and the map cannot be trusted. It's a fun and bracing read, a cool addition to the Fischer canon."
- *M.E. Proctor, author of the Declan Shaw series (USA)*

PRAISE FOR CORRECTION LINE

"Terlson captures the essence of life on the prairies: the barrenness, the isolated pockets of people, the strangeness that can be found hidden next to the normal. His attention to detail and style of writing drew me into the story and I felt like I was there."
- *C Neufeld (USA)*

"Dark, unique, oddly charming, occasionally bleak, and unexpected […] Terlson creates such supreme tension throughout the tale that you're never sure exactly when the next blow will fall."
- *Amy (CAN)*

"Terlson's writing brings up echos of Garcia Marquez and Allende, [all] while creating stunning slipstream prairie prose that are all his own."
- *Kirsten K (Kenya)*

SAYULITA SUCKER

CRAIG TERLSON

SAYULITA SUCKER

Ethelbert House

First Edition, 2025

Cover Design by Craig Terlson

Interior Design by Jourdan Dunn

ISBN: 978-1-7381036-5-2 (pbk)
ISBN: 978-1-7381036-4-5 (ebook)

KEN, KENNETH, MIKE, WHATEVER THE HELL YOUR NAME IS.
THIS ONE'S FOR YOU, BUDDY.

CHAPTER ONE

SOMETIMES THINGS ARE JUST DIFFERENT, and mostly that's okay. That's what I tell the crow who is staring me down from my chair in the Hotel Rosita. It's a perfect Mexican afternoon, the sun at the right angle and temperature to raise both a sweat and a thirst. The wind is picking up and the waves are rolling in, crashing like sticks on a high-hat. Damn if there isn't always a music to this place.

The black bird, as big as a small chicken, was perched on a leather-wrapped chair, identical to mine, complete with the requisite black dots punched into the upholstery. There was no doubt the bugger was judging me—or at least questioning. He knew something was off.

He and his winged buddies stalked the terra cotta tiles in the Rosita like they owned the goddamned place, and maybe they did. I'd named this one Phil after a Vietnam vet I had the somewhat pleasure of knowing before I found his corpse stretched out behind a shed in rural New Mexico. I always liked—no, check that, respected Phil. Hopefully, wherever he was playing his harp or twanging his pitchfork, he was pleased that I had named the cocky black bird after him. And if he didn't like it, well, the hell with Phil. I didn't respect him *that* much.

The crow was right to question me. The Rosita was not my usual perch. The hotel was almost toney by P.V. standards—outside comparing the spit-shined resorts that lined the north end of the city. But the orange-and-white tablecloths and the brick arches that encased the bar and restaurant were a lot better than my usual digs at the Esperanzo. That two-star wonder was about ten minutes up the hill, and I could sort of see the ocean from there if I got a room on a high enough floor. Here at the Rosita I not only heard but also saw the surf, those high-hat sounds mixed with the squawking birds who walked the walk. A jet-blue heron circled high above, ready to grab a fish or dive bomb a turista, whichever proved easier.

I reminded myself I was also a tourist here—feeling even more so in the Rosita. Still, I'd kicked around this country long enough to consider myself semi-local. I put the pat in ex-pat, whatever the fuck that meant.

I chomped on a plate of chips with a mound of excellent guac and small bowl of fresh, hot salsa dotted with chunks of white onion. I was on my third Tecate, another difference being the Rosita was out of Pacificos. Who the hell runs out of Pacificos? You can throw a rock and hit one of their sunshine-yellow trucks that peel around the city. Still, Tecate in an ice-chilled mug with a couple of wedges of lime would do fine on this hot Puerta Vallarta afternoon.

Benno was away on business this week, which could mean any number of legal or illegal things. If he was around, I would have asked him about the guy who set me up at the Rosita. I got rousted out of my bed at the crack of noon by one of the Esperanzo staff, telling me I had a phone call. The guy on the phone sprinkled enough Spanish between his English that in my sleepy state I had to keep asking him to repeat himself. He was a business associate of Benno's. When I pressed him on that, I didn't get much else. He wouldn't even give his name.

"I have arranged a room for you at the Hotel Rosita. It is one of the city's best. The camarones there are excellent."

He told me he was going to be arriving the next day, but I was welcome to stay at the Rosita. Benno must have told him how to find me, and I guess he didn't want to meet me at the Esperanzo. He said he would introduce himself properly when we met. He sounded like he was on the toney side and wouldn't darken the door of my usual digs. I recalled my convo with Benno when I'd first got back into the city two weeks ago.

"You know they painted the tower green," I'd told Benno. "The place is really spruced up."

"That is a funny word, my friend," Benno said. "Spruce, like the tree. Is this something they say in Canada?"

"Just the lumberjacks."

Benno gave a nod that I came to learn meant he didn't understand what I said, nor did he care.

"The Esperanzo is a fine and honest place, and I'm glad you are finding a home there, Luke."

He was right about that. The Esperanzo did feel like home. But the room at the Rosita was pleasant, the bed soft, and the decor matched the blankets. The morning breakfast was huevos rancheros with chiles Christmas-style. Once again, no surprise to me, I was hungover. I ate so much I needed to head back to bed with a cup of cinnamon-laced coffee and read a John D. book until I nodded off. I woke up around three, thinking I could get used to this luxury. My head was still doing the rhumba, and I gave some thought to whether I should leave my bed. But I needed to meet this guy in the lounge.

I'd been waiting two hours for the associate to show at the Rosita, and in spite of last night, I was thinking of switching to tequila. It was expensive by the glass here, but what did I care if this guy was picking up the tab. Still, if I moved over to the agave plant at this time of day, I'd soon be in no shape to hold a business meeting. I didn't know what the guy wanted to talk about, but if he was involved with Benno, I needed to have at least some of my wits in check.

A thin, well-dressed man entered the lobby and stopped at the desk. The young kid with a missing tooth and a wide smile whose name I learned was Carlos pointed over to the lounge. The man had a neatly trimmed goatee. I figured he was the one looking for me, so I waved him over.

"Buenos dias. You are señor Fischer?"

"That's what my driver's license says."

"I don't understand. I am not in need of a driver."

I gestured to the seat across from me Phil the Crow had just vacated. "Sit."

"I am a friend of señor Benno," he said.

"Friend or associate?"

"Again, I am not sure I understand."

"On the phone you were an associate, now you're moved up to friend."

The man stroked his beard in that annoying way that people who like their facial hair do.

"If I am inconveniencing you, señor Fischer, I will take my leave."

"Where will you take it?"

The man stood to leave.

"Oh, sit back down. I got a bit testy waiting for you."

"I'm not sure I know this word, but I do apologize for my lateness. My driver fell ill, and I decided to travel by bus."

"Why not hire a car?"

"As a boy I would ride the Centro bus all the time, often for free. I thought I might relive that experience again."

The thin man's accent was light, he obviously knew his way around English. Though not its crazy idioms like *testy*. But who was I to talk? I could barely order a cerveza and a plate of camarones without sounding like I had a mouthful of sand.

"So what can I do for you señor, uh…" I held my hand open.

"Have you spoken with señor Benno?" He glanced back at the lobby like he expected my benefactor to come waltzing in.

"No. He's out of town, or maybe the country."

"I see."

Again with the check back.

"You expecting someone else?"

"No. I am distracted, that is all."

"Well, spit it out."

"It is a sensitive matter."

"A lot of matters are," I said. "Look, if you don't want to tell me your name, that's fine."

"You may call me Morales. Hectore, if you wish."

That sounded like a fake name right from the get-go.

"Okay, Hector."

"Hectore."

"Right. Hectore," I let the "o" ring in my mouth. "We have the niceties out of the way. What do you want?"

"Benno did not tell me of your rudeness."

I sighed and pinched my nose between my eyes. This wouldn't be happening if they hadn't run out of Pacificos.

"Again, if I am inconv—"

"Knock it off. Let's cut to it."

Morales fumbled with his tie, a nice silk job. He looked tired—from more than a bus ride on P.V.'s fine transportation system. A bubble of empathy appeared in my head, but I popped it.

"Mi hija."

He said it so quietly, his words almost disappeared in the breeze. A crow squawked. It could have been Phil. It sounded like him.

"My Spanish is not the greatest, Hectore." This was a lie—it was actually really shitty. "Something about your son?"

"Mi hija," he started. "My daughter. She has gone."

"Gone like dead?"

He collapsed his face into his hands. "No, no, no."

"Look, I'm sorry, Hectore. Uh, Morales. I don't mean to— "

He brought his red eyes up to me. "That is what I have feared. But I know in my heart, a father knows, that she is still alive. But I have not heard from her for almost a month."

"Oh. Gone like that."

"Yes. Señor Benno said that you would help me. He said that you were very good at finding those who are lost or missing. He said you were an excellent detective. Can I purchase your services?"

"Sorry, not a detective."

"Then you are not for hire?"

"I didn't say that."

"I will pay handsomely."

"I figured you would."

CHAPTER TWO

"SO IF YOUR DAUGHTER is missing, go to the policía. I can tell you've got the kind of dough to get somebody to care."

Morales stood to leave. "I thank you for your time, señor Fischer."

"Oh, sit down, Morales. I'm just in a mood."

"Call me Hectore. And I don't know what you mean by this mood."

"Tell you what, I'm gonna call you Morales. And you're buying the next round. I'd take a Pacifico but for some goddamn reason they are out."

"Corona?" Morales eyebrows rose.

"Donkey piss. I'll take a Tecate, two of them. And a plate of tostados ceviche."

"A good choice on a hot day. The pescado refreshes."

Morales gave our order to the waiter in the red jacket. He ordered himself a Modelo. Everything at the Rosita was a step up from what I was used to. But they were a friendly lot, and they didn't bother me every ten minutes like one of the palapas on the beach.

"How long?" I asked Morales.

"For the cerveza?"

"Your daughter. How long has she been gone?"

Morales spilled out his tale like it had been bottled up in him too long and he had finally popped the cork.

"Slow down. And don't mix the Spanish with the English. I'll have a better chance of understanding."

The beers and ceviche came as Morales talked. The tangy fish, veggie, and lime mixture burnt the sides of my mouth in the best way; the cooks had snuck in some chilies with all the acid. It was fiery, but Hectore was right. It was refreshing as hell. I finished one Tecate and tucked into the next.

The daughter had been gone a month now. Morales last saw her at his home down in Conchas Chinas. Locals called this neighborhood "The Hills," as in the Beverly Hills of P.V. I was right. Hectore must be loaded.

"How did she seem?" I asked.

"Seem?"

"You know what I'm asking. With you?"

"Yes." He plucked at his beard. "You are wondering how the two of us got along. As you have guessed, my daughter has been rebelling against me for a number of years. Since her mother, may she rest in peace, passed, I spent too much time in my work. But it was necessary for me or else be swallowed by grief."

"How did your wife die?"

"She was sick with cancer, but that was not the end."

Morales took a long pull on his beer and grimaced.

"Heart gave out? That's what happened to my old man. Got him before the cancer could do him in. Died walking up the stairs."

"You witnessed this?"

"What about your wife?"

"She did not wait for the cancer to, as you say, do her in."

"No offence, Morales. Death of any kind is a kick in the head."

"She walked off the balcony and fell into the ocean below."

"She drowned?"

"I am certain the rocks killed before her skin was even wet." Morales straightened his tie and cleared his throat. "Can you help me, señor Fischer? I am in need of a detective. My daughter has been in trouble with los federales a number of times. They will not care if she is found. Alive, or…" He didn't finish.

Dammit if that bubble didn't appear again.

"Sorry, Morales. For everything, I mean. But I'm not a detective," I said.

"But señor Benno said you would help. I will pay you well. He is a friend, a good friend of mine, and he will confirm that I am to be trusted." Morales looked over at the front desk. I cranked my head around to see what he saw, but it was just Carlos reading a magazine. "Although he may be hard to reach now."

"Why is that?"

"As you said. Señor Benno is out of the country."

The sun started its dip in the Pacific, orange reflections spread out like syrup on a glass plate. An especially good sunset this evening. Two pelicans dove, their splashes making ripples in the syrup. A heron had been circling high above the Rosita. I'd spied him when I was talking with Phil the Crow. But I didn't want to mention the magnificent bird to Phil in case birds had their own inferiority complexes. The heron started a low dive now, skimming the water and coming up with a fat fish. The pelicans looked like they came up empty, staring in envy at their sleek, faster pal.

I watched the light slide down the white walls of the Rosita.

"Señor?"

I held up my hand to Morales. This was a time for quiet. A pair of small children splashed in the pool, their chitters matching the bird-song.

In his story, Morales had told me his daughter had friends in Bucerias, a beach town barely thirty minutes north. As close as it was, I'd never spent any time there.

"You think she might be with these friends up in Bucerias?"

"You will take my case, Mr. Fischer?"

"It's Mr. now? Huh. And case, God no. I hate the sound of that. But I'll poke around."

"Señor Benno said that when you worked you are like a wolf with a bone."

"A dog?"

"I believe he said wolf. So you will help me?"

"I've heard Bucerias has some pretty decent fish tacos."

Morales stared at me like I was speaking a language neither of us knew.

"She also had a boyfriend," he started. "Like you, he was from the United States, with long hair and tattoos that wrap around his legs like thick vines. He is a surfer."

"Yeah, no doubt. And I'm not from the U.S."

"I am sorry for the assumption," Morales said.

"The boyfriend hang out in Sayulita?"

"Yes. I believe he does. How did you know?"

"Good guess around here. That's where a lot of long-haired surfers end up. Sayulita has some of the best waves. Throw a rock and you hit a Californian."

"I see." My table partner squinted and tapped his fingers on the rim of his Modelo.

"What's her name? Her real name, Hectore?" I put an emphasis on the last syllable, which cause Morales to give a snort somewhere between a swallow and a hiccup.

"I am sorry, Mr. Fischer. I have not been honest with you."

"No shit."

He rubbed his eyes and gave the beard another pull. "My name is Ramone."

"Ramone what?"

"Morales is my family name. I am not sure why I hid this from you."

"Benno would have wondered."

"Yes. You are correct. My daughter's name is Agnacia, but she is often called Soleil."

I considered this. It seemed like Ramone was laying it out.

"Ha. So she is your sun, then."

"Ah, yes. That is why they call her that. She is full of life. Beautiful. Radiant is a good word."

"Yeah it is."

"I deeply appreciate your help Mr. Fischer."

"Call me Luke."

"It is a good name."

"You got a picture of your daughter?"

"Of course."

He took out a black leather wallet and slid out a square photo, black-and-white, like from one of those booths where you take them yourself. Even in gray, her face shone, smiling as if she'd just heard a joke. I wondered who told it.

CHAPTER THREE

"OKAY, RAMONE, I'll take a bus up to Bucerias and see if I can find any trace of Sunny."

"Soleil."

"Right."

"Why not hire a driver? I will pay for these expenses. Señor Benno speaks very highly of you."

"Probably too highly. Anyway, I prefer the segunda. Slower ride, easier pace."

"But I do wish to find my daughter. There is that saying about time being the essence. Are you aware?"

"Yeah, I've heard that one."

"I'm afraid what she might have found her way into." Morales's eye twitched like a bug had flown into it.

"She's been gone a month. A few more hours won't hurt."

More twitches. I looked around for a swarm.

"You will leave right away?"

"Sure."

I shouldn't be so pissy with the guy—but the pounding surf inside my head reminded me of how many tequilas I had the night before. Well, not the exact number. But it was Hornitas. Or something brown and horny. I really needed to stay away from that stuff.

"Mr. Fischer?"

"What happened to señor?"

The bottom of Morales's eyes were red and watery. Dammit if I didn't reach across and pat his hands.

"I'll see what I can do, Morales." I swallowed some spit from last night. "I apologize for my mood. I didn't sleep well. I never do."

"Ramone. Call me Ramone."

"Okay, Morales." I patted his hands one more time. "I'll finish this plate of ceviche and one more cerveza. Two, tops. And then I'll head to Bucerias."

Morales looked like he wanted to ask another question, but I grabbed his hand and gave an awkward handshake combination head-nod-no-talking signal. I was using all the body language I knew to get him to leave the Rosita and let me get back to my drinking.

"Here is card with my direct line. Call me as soon as you find her. I will take care of the bill."

"I expect you will," I said.

"When we talk next, I will let you know if I have found anything out."

"Yeah. You keep looking, and I'll do the same." I touched my forehead with my index and gave it a flip.

Morales seemed to study my faux-salute and then left. I watched him hand a card to a jacketed waiter.

I finish the ceviche and order two more Tecates. My pounding head has softened with the acidy fish and the pleasing hops. I might survive the day.

The Rosita was half-full. Gringos and locales were spread out at the tables. Being the oldest hotel in P.V., it still attracted Mexicans on vacation, though much cheaper places could be found. The Esperanza was always good enough for me.

I had my eye on a sun-burned gringo in a green straw hat. The hat was sweat-stained, and he scribbled furiously into a small book. Huh. A would-be writer, or maybe a real one. Who knew? I was wondering what stories he told of this place when a hand came down hard on my shoulder.

"Fisch-man! How the hell are you, amigooo?" He stretched out the O like he was announcing a goal in a European football match.

I knew the voice before he waltzed around and sat across from me. Bob Sokan from Indiana or Illinois or somewhere with an "I."

"Hey, Bob. Been in town for a while?"

"Long enough to dance through the diarrhea shuffle."

"Nice image, Bob."

"What are you doing in this joint, Fisch-cat? Above your standards. Aren't you usually up the hill in some local shithole?"

"Easy, Bob. I'm not in the best of moods."

"Ha." His laugh was like a fork-stab in the head. "Since when are you ever in a good mood?"

"There was that one time," I said. "I think it was a Thursday."

Bob's voice and cologne were too loud for the place. The Loud American is a badge Bob wears with pride. I've met lots of Americans who weren't like this, but Bob wears his badge with more honor than a sheriff from Dodge City.

"I'd buy you a beer, Fisch-dude. But I gotta see a man about a horse."

"You have to take a piss, just go."

"Ha! No, an actual horse. I never thought of that, good one." He reached across, and I ducked out of the way of his playful punch. "I've been dealing on a couple of beauties over in Bucerias. You ever been on that stretch? Flat as fuck, and the waves roll in like the red carpet."

"Carpet?"

"Or whatever. What the hell do I know? I'm from Nebraska."

I could have sworn it was an I-place.

"Sounds like you're on a mission, Bob."

"Hey Fisch-Bird, what are you doing at the Rooosita?" Bob laughed at his rolling r's. "You meeting a little piece?"

"Just taking it in."

"Ah. El secreto." He did a finger flip off his nose. "Listen, you get up to Bucerias, look me up at the Los Picos. I'll buy you whatever you're drinking."

Bob bolted up, shook my hand too hard, and tilted his hat.

"Whattya want with a horse, Bob?"

"Hmm? Oh just buying and selling. It's what I do, man. It's the Mexican way."

There was a light in Bob's eyes that could be the sun or could be him playing fast and loose with the truth. Never did trust Nebraska-Bob

—too many caps on his teeth. The sparkle was hiding something gritty underneath. But like Bob, what the hell did I know?

If I'd told him I was also going to Bucerias, he'd probably give me a lift. But I'd rather drop the twenty pesos and get a segunda bus-window view of the landscape. Also, I wouldn't have to listen to Bob talk about horses. I let him leave the Rosita without saying where I was headed.

Phil was back, and the cheeky bastard hopped right on the table and squawked at me.

"Well, fuck you too, buddy."

Phil gave another squawk.

"Listen, it's your round this time, and I'll tell you right now they don't take seeds at the bar."

Phil leapt off the table and hopped in and out of the orange shadows. I finished one of the Tecates and reached for the second, the bottle already dripping condensation.

I guess I needed the work. It would probably pay well. And helping Benno was always in my best interest, if he really was pals with Morales. *Dammit.* I wanted to get a hold of him to ask, but I knew that when Benno left town, he was impossible to reach.

I had to think this one through, which meant I needed a long walk. Better, a run, to sweat out some of the alcohol. Doing a quick body check, I turned that idea down as fast it came into my head.

"Phil, save my seat."

I tossed a hundred pesos on the table and weaved my way out of the Rosita.

Evenings always came on fast in P.V. As soon as the sun was down, the air started to cool and the lights came on in the clubs that lined the Malecón. The usual vendors and doormen called over, beckoning me to try some tequila, or a cigar, or take a tour somewhere. Since I'd hung my nonexistent hat in this city, I'd grown both used to the verbal barrage and tired of it at the same time. I veered off the Malecón and walked up a street that grew quieter the farther I got from the beach. Guitar strings were being plucked somewhere, either in a small club or my imagination.

A thin guy in a baggy coat approached me.

"Mota."

I waved him off. The last thing I needed was weed to clog up my already fuzzy head.

"Cremita, señor?"

He grabbed my shoulder and tugged. I pushed him off, my shoulders immediately tensed. I wasn't in the mood for a street fight, but one more aggressive move from the guy and I'd give him a swat. Of course, if he was selling coke, he was probably using it, and those thin ones were the druggies to watch out for. Wiry bastards had reflexes like alley cats.

"Buenas nochas," he said and sulked away.

Damn. How hard was it to find a place to think around here?

Already, a couple of stars had winked on and a creamy moon climbed the purple sky. The sweat had dried off my neck, and there was a cool breeze wafting behind me, like it was urging me into the night.

The guy's daughter sounded findable—or she could be drugged out, or up, whatever they're calling it these days. Maybe living in psychedelic la-la land with a couple of aging surfers from Huntington Beach with skin as weathered as their flip-flops. Or she could be dead. If that was the case, I'd be the son of a bitch who found out.

Turned out the music I'd heard wasn't in my imagination. Warm light spilled onto the street from an open door. A row of four chairs lined the wall on either side of the door. Three were empty, but the fourth held an old man smoking a thin cigarette, his head swayed, barely perceptible, to the beat that drifted from inside the small club. He touched his hat and then waved an arm, inviting me inside.

"Buenas noches." His voice was deep, and it fit perfectly in with the melody being played, like he had waited for the perfect moment to say it.

The club looked to be filled mostly with locals, maybe too far off the main track for the turistas to venture. There was a couple near the front huddled around one of the small tables, transfixed by the guitar player and his vocalist who were both perched on tall stools. Usually I'd hear chatter rising and falling in a small place like this, but they were all listening. I could see why. The sounds were gentle, like lapping waves. The singer's voice wove over the warm tones plucked by the guitarist.

A woman with flowing hair turned, noticing me standing in the middle of the room, and extended her hand to the empty chair beside her. I nodded and joined her. She smiled, then closed her eyes and swayed her head like the elderly doorman who had waved me in. I closed my eyes and dipped into the surf.

I'd had nights similar to this one, where I found myself in a place that didn't seem quite real. I guess the psychologists would call it surreal. It didn't matter. Years ago, a friend returned from a trip across the pond, Scotland, I thought. He described to me the time he'd spent in the thin places.

"Thin? Like a narrow street?" I'd asked.

"It's a place where our world bumps up against the next one."

My friend wasn't a churchgoer, nor had he ever talked about other worlds.

"You talking the afterlife, or Jesus, Heaven? Like pearly gates and shit?"

He held a single finger to his lips. "Luke, we walk around this ball, thinking it's what is real. Ground under our feet, cars, buildings, and people selling things. We think this is it. But over there, you come up against some place where you can feel the other place."

I never knew what he meant or experienced anything like it. Until this night.

Hours stretched out, I don't even know how many. I was drinking, eating, breathing, doing all the things I usually do. But in a way I wasn't. My table partner's name was Alicia. She didn't speak much English, but she didn't need to. When the last song of the night finished, she walked me into the still P.V. night. A pale moon stared down from the indigo sky. I felt like I could reach up and pull a chain to shut it off. She took my hand, and we went down the hill together; even the cobblestones seemed smoother.

The beach was empty, another strange sight, but sometimes things shut down early. Especially in the middle of the week, if that's what it was. Without a warning, she gave me a long, lingering kiss. Pulling away gently, she whispered, "Buenas noches."

Then she walked away into the night. At some point the moon went out, and I found my way back to the Rosita.

CHAPTER FOUR

I AWOKE EARLIER than I should have after a night that still seemed dreamlike. I wasn't hungover, which was a nice change of pace. I had one of those hummingbird thoughts that said I should cut back on the cerveza and late-night tequila sessions. I told the bird to get ripped and made my way downstairs in search of a cup of cinnamon-laced brew. The lounge doubled as the breakfast area, but the place was almost empty, and a couple of the staff were already cleaning up the long food table. I grabbed a sweet bun and a slice of pineapple, poured a to-go, and left the hotel.

The sun blazed down on my head and made me think, not for the first time, that I really should start wearing a hat. Benno had a good idea there, as did that sunburned scribbler yesterday in the Rosita lounge, not that it did him any good. That sort of guy needed a good layer of sunscreen or maybe just to stay inside.

I chomped on my breakfast and then rebalanced it on my cup, a skill I'd acquired over many mornings. I use the word morning loosely, since I saw the sun had already climbed close to the noon slot, and the heat of the day rose to meet it. A layer of sweat crawled across my neck as I sauntered to the bus stop. A couple of men had followed me out of the Rosita. They were most likely locals or Mexican vacationers who like me were looking to get out of town or score a bus that had some A.C. None of the city buses were cooled, and when I transferred to one of the second-class jobs, the segundas, it was a long shot that they'd have anything more air-cooling than a cracked window. But I might get to sit next to a chicken. Somehow that seemed more real to me. They never complained about the heat either.

I got on a Centro bus, along with the two that had come over from the Rosita. I wasn't paranoid enough to think they were following me. Or not yet anyway. The ride over the P.V. cobblestones jarred my bones. The too-sweet pastry and acidy-pineapple performed loops in my stomach that'd make Flipper jealous. I pushed open the window and was rewarded with a blast of hot afternoon air. A woman weighed down with her daily shopping bags squeezed in next to me. She smelled of oranges and some sort of spice I could place. It wasn't unpleasant.

I hadn't really planned on hitting the road in the heat of the day. I'd been looking forward to a long dip in the pool, followed by more drinking. But dammit if I didn't have a job to do—so instead I was headed out on what already seemed like a mission of futility. I made a note to talk with Benno when he got back. Just what was his actual relationship with Ramone Morales? I didn't doubt there was one, otherwise I would have accepted Morales picking up the bill and made my way back to the Esperanzo. Still, there was something burbling underneath my new employer, and I'd like the full story.

It was probably the two stragglers from the Rosita that had flipped a couple of the suspicion switches that had me thinking about Morales. I'd been lied to too many times, on both sides of the border, not to question the supposed truth.

I got off the Centro and moved to the long bus shelter already lined with people waiting for their connections. One of the Rosita men followed me; the other stayed on the bus. This part of the city was one of the busiest sections of P.V. Over the stretch of multilane road hung a chalk-white walking bridge. A couple of kids leaned over the speeding traffic. One hawked a big loogie onto the road, and they threw their heads back and laughed in unison. Not a bad way to spend a day.

The white segundas pulled up next to the shelter, town names written on their windshields. I waited until one with "Bucerias" showed up. I took a fast glance at my travelling companion, but he'd already lined up to the bus behind the one I was getting on. His was headed to Sayulita and San Pancho. A muscle in the back of my neck released.

"Cuánto cuesta Bucerias?"

"Sesenta."

I gave the driver a hundred, he did a fast clack on his change machine, and handed me some coins. Before I found a seat in the back, he'd already lurched into traffic and gunned it. I fought the urge to paint the bus with my looping breakfast and memories of pescado-laden ceviche before grabbing a seat-back and swiveling into it. I pushed on the narrow window, and it might have been my imagination or wishful thinking, but a stream of cool breeze wafted through to me. I slunk down in the seat. Music drifted through the bus and mixed with the traffic noises outside. It was some kind of Mexican groove-pop. Drums whacked a steady beat and a guitar cut through in a groovy rift that would have made Dick Dale proud. I wished the tunes would drown out the cars, and as if the driver was reading my mind, the volume increased.

My guts had started to settle, and I slipped into a deep sleep, falling into one of the recurring surfer dreams I'd been having lately. A Spanish singer urged me on as I paddled out to a line of rolling Pacific waves. The bay moved from what the surfers called corduroy into some cranking waves. I was up and easily riding high on top of a beauty. It curled into a pipeline, and I crouched down, shooting down the tunnel of churning green-blue water. I had one of those realizations you get while dreaming that I really didn't know how to surf—even if I'd watched many young tanned men slalom the waves in Barra de Navidad. Hey, shit, a guy could dream.

I bolted up in the seat and looked outside. I had no idea how long I was out. I knew the drive to Bucerias wasn't that long, less than an hour. I weaved up to the front of the bus and spoke to the driver.

"Bucerias?"

He didn't look up at me.

"Mande?"

"The town, Bucerias, did we pass it?"

"Que?"

This time he glanced over, looking at me like a fly that buzzed around his head.

"Bucerias, por favor?" I tried my best to sound less like a pain in the ass.

A nod of recognition, and then a thumb jab to somewhere behind me. Obviously, we'd already gone by and I slept through the stop, if he even did stop. I knew without asking he wasn't going to turn around, and if I got him to pull over, I had no clue how many miles I'd have to walk to Bucerias.

"Sayulita?"

His eyes were back on the road. The driver pointed ahead. I hesitated, considered giving him more money, but realized he didn't give a shit. I went back to my seat and settled in for the rest of the ride to Sayulita. Oh well, I'd figured on going there anyway to see if I could track down Sunny's surfing boyfriend. I could always catch Bucerias on my way back, if there seemed a reason to do so. It was a good question for this whole thing I was doing. Why do something instead of nothing?

CHAPTER FIVE

I KNEW OF SAYULITA and the surfing mecca it was supposed to be, but I'd never spent any time there. A while back, I'd passed it on my way to P.V., but I was coming from the other direction. Worried I'd miss the damn town again, I got off a stop much too early and hoofed it the rest of the way. The sun had not lessened in intensity, and once again I swore I was going to find a Benno-worthy fedora. I'd seen a map of Nayarit at a coffeehouse in P.V. hanging over a shelf of dusty paperbacks. I recalled that Sayulita was on an angle, wrapped around the Pacific coastline—but Mr. and Mrs. Fischer had never blessed their son with a good sense of direction, so I couldn't put my mind's faded image together with the actual geography of where I stood. Dusty roads arrowed off in different directions, and I had no idea where the ocean was. It was a big fucking thing, blue and wet. Shouldn't be so hard to find.

The small shops along the road I walked on were closed, maybe for siesta, or maybe business was just too slow to stay open. A boy on a bike rode up to me.

"Hey kid, where's the ocean?"

He looked at me like I was the dumbest thing in town. And maybe I was.

"Que?"

"Ocean. Damn. Playa. Donde esta la?"

The kid smirked. A line of dirt ran from his nose and disappeared under his Thriller t-shirt. He must have worn that thing every damn day, given the threadbare condition it was in. I figured he was figuring on whether to tell the gringo anything. He reached out his hand, and I fished in my pocket for the pair of twenty-peso coins. The kid rolled them in his hand, jerked a thumb behind him, and rode off.

"Yeah, well, *Off the Wall* was his best album, ya little shit!"

The boy had pointed in the direction I was already going, so I went with it. A number of streets spidered off the main drag; I just had to decide which one to take. As I walked, the streets got busier, and more gringos like me appeared alongside the locals. I'd been in Mexico long enough to no longer consider myself a gringo, which was always a mistake, because I always would be. A tall, skinny dude the color of shoe leather slid past with a bright lemon-colored surfboard. Another skinnier and even more leather-like guy joined him with a powder-blue board.

When in doubt, follow the surfers. I needed that on a goddamn t-shirt.

As I followed the men with boards, the street grew more crowded. People in various shades of baked skin emerged from the rows of shops. These vendors, unlike the ones I'd passed, were hopping. The surfer, or surfer wannabes, were dressed in cut-off jeans, muscle shirts that showed off their toned bodies, and sun-bleached hair, or at least drugstore-dyed. Others wore shorts the color of sherbet, a few with translucent skin and knobby knees, what the veteran surfers would have called Barneys—their derogatory word for rookies. A slick dude in a lime-green number haggled with a salesman next to a row of vertical boards. The sun glinted off the thick-waxed surfaces.

Down a few wooden stairs, the dirt turned to a burnt grassy trail and then to sand. The sound of people rose with the waves that crashed along the coast. I stood on the beach and watched a half dozen surfers ride the water. I'd done this often down in Barra Navidad so many times that I knew right away the ones who were pros, or at least damn good. I used to think surfing was all about catching those big monster waves, like in the opening to *Hawaii Five-O*. A convo I had with a tanned man, age unknown, on a rock in Barra changed my mind. The waves that day were plentiful, but, in my uninformed mind, on the small side.

"Not too much to ride on out there," I said to him.

He'd climbed up on a rock next to mine, unwrapped a bright papaya, and chomped into it. Through a mouth full of fruit, he schooled me.

"Too many say if the waves are too small it is not worth it."

"You a surfer?"

"Not any more. But I still know there are many lessons to be learned in the tiny ripples."

I considered this, obviously with the *Five-O* theme playing in my head.

"I thought it was all about catching the big ones."

He pointed with his juice-covered hand to the ocean. "A large wave will do everything for you. A small breaker makes you work."

"Why would you want to work?" I asked.

"A fine but also a dumb question."

He didn't mean it as an insult; it was like he was thinking of the reason himself, not just in surfing but in life.

"With a small wave, you are always adjusting. The subtlest body adjustments will keep the board gliding through the water."

As he spoke, one of the surfers did exactly what he said, cutting and swooping, then sliding effortlessly into shore. It was beautiful to watch.

"Like that?" I pointed.

"Like that," he said, then wrapped the black seeds in a white cloth and left me on the rock to think about the lesson.

Right now, there was a young woman on a lemon-yellow board doing just what my rock-tutor had told me. She was easily the best out there. I admired skill like that and the hours it must have taken to perfect. It made me want to be better at what I did—even though I didn't do much.

I made my way to a row of blue chairs that gave a great view of the dozen or so surfers riding the crests. As soon as I plunked down, a man in a large straw hat appeared. Written in a thick black scrawl across the brim was the word "SONNY."

"A beautiful view on a beautiful day, señor."

"Are you Sonny?"

"Yes. I am. And for the small price of three hundred pesos, you can enjoy this view for four hours. Five hundred pesos for the entire day. You can watch the sun dip into the water. If you listen closely, you will hear it."

Sun bounced off his too-white teeth.

"It costs to sit here?"

I looked up the beach, which was clogged with many of the same chairs, and men and woman in similar hats wove in and out of the rows.

"Those other places are not near as good. Here you will have Sonny's excellent service. I will bring you whatever you need. Cerveza, Tequila, tostados— "

"And what does it cost to sit over there?"

I pointed at a dark wooden structure surrounded by greenery farther down the beach and perched on a small incline.

"To really experience Sayulita, señor, you need to be on the beach, like the locals. Like Sonny." Again with the wide smile.

By the looks of it, most of the crowd was made up of what I assumed were Californians who'd drifted down here in their Westfalias and never left.

"I'll give the other place a go, Sonny. Maybe I'll be back."

"I'll try to save this one for you, but I cannot guarantee."

I gave the chair salesman a wave and made my way to the beach bar. Inside, the foliage and dark wood made it seem a few degrees cooler, and I appreciated the reprieve from the heat. Large, open floor-to-straw ceiling windows looked over the ocean surf.

A guy with a black felt hat, wrapped in a dirty pink bandana, wove through the bar strumming a worn guitar and singing. He wore a black cloth vest over his pink shirt. He wasn't feeling the heat like I was. By his side was a lithe, tanned woman with striking blue eyes that matched her gorgeous white smile. Mexico must have some good dentists.

The woman held a shaker or a maraca, whatever they call those things. She shook along with her partner's playing and periodically sang some "ooos" in warm harmony. The guitar player had a pan flute in a cotton sleeve that hung around his neck. He blew, soft breathy notes, and the music mixed with the surf and gulls drifting from the beach. The whole effect made me relaxed as hell. A guy like me could spend some hours here, maybe the whole day.

"Pacifico?" I asked the woman in a red apron who handed me a paper menu.

"Si. Uno?"

"Better make it dos." I held up two fingers, then turned and pointed to the musicians who had slid into another number, or had simply continued the first. "They're really good," I said, but she was no longer there.

* * *

THE BEERS CAME WITH A SMALL PLATE of chips, salsa, and wedges of lime crowded into a white bowl. I knew I was supposed to be making a plan, talking to some people, figuring shit out, but I was having a lot of motivational issues today, or this week, or month.

"Señor?"

A rotund man with a bushy moustache held a wooden case in front of him full of four-packs of cigars. I recognized the bands, Cohiba, Romeo y Julieta, Montecristo. If they were the real deal, they'd be worth a few bucks. I waved him off, but then he did a little dance with his head in perfect time with the strumming.

"It is a beautiful day for cold cervezas, beautiful music, and ocean air. What would be better than to enjoy a cigar?"

"No thanks. I'm good just sitting here."

"Of course you are. Cómo te llamas, señor?"

"Fischer."

He kept doing his dance while he talked, now getting his shoulders into it.

"A very good price for such a good name. Two for one," he said.

"Cubans?"

"But of course. You come from America, where you can't get such a fine smoke."

"I live here now," I said.

"But not always."

"Canada."

He broke into a wide smile, bright teeth shining through the thick hedge of a moustache. Damn, I needed to brush my own more often.

"Allow me to join you for a moment, señor?"

"Why?"

"I have something that may interest you."

"I'm not interested in the cigars. I gave them up. Too hard on the lungs."

He closed his case, latched it, and put it under my table. He slid out one of the heavy chairs wrapped in straw and dark cords, then plunked down across from me.

"I see why you came. This is a place of rest. Too much sun and noise out there." He pointed out the open-air window. Like he planned it, a passel of children ran across the beach, tipping over those expensive beach chairs that Sonny was selling.

"I thought you said it was beautiful?"

He laughed. "I like you Canadians. You are much more relaxed than the Yankees. And funny, you are very funny."

"It's all the snow and hockey," I said.

My cigar-selling friend gave a quizzical look. "I sell much more than cigars."

"I never had any doubt," I said.

"I have marijuana, or something stronger, the white powder? You know it." He must have thought he saw something on my face. "Aha, so that is it."

"What's your name?" I asked.

"Que?"

"Te llamas?"

"Oh, me? Your Spanish is very good," he lied. "I am Lopez, like the great fighter. You've heard of him?"

"I have. Now listen, Lopez. I just want to sit in this nice shady bar, drink my beer, and watch the seagulls. I'm not in the market for anything else."

As I talked, my new table friend started bopping his head to the soft guitar rhythm. It would have pissed me off, but damn if I didn't start doing it, too. Then, like someone threw a switch, the music stopped.

"I can get you a woman."

He said it quietly—a good thing, because the whole place had gone strangely silent after the musicians quit their set. No applause, not even the usual bar murmurs.

"What?"

Lopez cranked his head around and gestured to the guitar player, who was moving from table to table with his bandana hat in hand. The musician nodded, accepted a few more bills in his hat, and then came over. Lopez gestured, and the guitarist leaned down. He studied me as Lopez spoke in his ear. At one point, he glanced over at his lovely percussionist, who was also making the rounds. She gave a smile and a wink, but I saw something flash across her face.

Before the musician left, he extended his hand, and I shook it.

"You play really well," I said.

"Muchas gracias."

Something tapped at the base of my neck. It could be just the heat of the day and the bus ride catching up with me, but I'd learned to pay attention to those sensations. It wasn't spider-senses or something goofy like that, but it was like I had my own small guitar player plucking strings in my head. The music had shifted into a minor key. I'd wandered into something that was more than the usual drugs and prostitutes.

"Sorry Lopez, I'm not interested in—"

"When I explain the situation, you may be." The cigar-seller's smile was gone, and damned if that caterpillar over his top lip didn't look darker.

The tapping turned into a small flame, then it was gone. I guess it was time to get into it.

CHAPTER SIX

A WIND BLEW THROUGH the beach bar. It had a cold edge to it, and as though it pulled the clouds along with it, the sky darkened. I gave my head a shake, wondering if I was imagining all of this. Sunny as hell Sayulita was suddenly covered in a long sheet of greyness. The universe was either trying to tell me something, or I needed another Pacifico.

My cigar-selling buddy Lopez was droning on about something, the landscape, the beach, some friend who sold fish from a dock. I had no idea what he was going on about. He dropped in Spanish phrases, which didn't help. That chilly wind and the nerve that plucked down my back told me I needed to pay attention. I'd come to Sayulita looking for a woman, hadn't I?

"I have heard things about you Canadians. But I cannot recall the word. You are…"

"Polite?"

"No, amigo. This has to do with sex."

I signaled the women in red for another Pacifico, changed my mind, and held up two fingers.

"You must have heard wrong," I said.

"I believe you are a man that would appreciate a young woman."

"How young?"

Lopez heard the disgust in my voice. "No. No. Not like that. We are not pigs."

Part of me wanted Lopez to leave right now, or, better, twenty minutes ago. But again, I remembered Morales and why I'd come here. Damned if I could avoid something that waltzed in and sat across from me with a case of fake cigars. The server brought me the Pacificos. She looked for a moment at Lopez, obviously recognizing him. He gave a nod, and she shrugged and muttered something in Spanish before quickly turning away.

"You're known here," I said.

Music drifted in the bar, this time not live, but rather a tinny radio sound. A mournful singer cooed over minor chords and soft percussion.

"I'm known many places," Lopez said.

He let that hang for a bit as we both listened to the music.

"Okay, you're not a pig. Who are you?"

The broad smile returned, even broader than before. "We have young women, pretty women." Lopez's tone dropped. "Very much wanting to please."

"Only because you make them."

Lopez clucked his tongue. "They choose this life." He leaned in too close. "Perhaps they are fond of the … nose powder … is that what you call it? You know this slang?"

"Sure."

I looked past Lopez through the open-air windows to the surf. The waves had increased in size. I couldn't see the woman on the lemon board from here. A muscular teen in crimson shorts flipped and face-planted into the ocean. The wave went over him like he wasn't even there.

"I am sorry, I have forgotten your name, señor."

"So you have."

A small laugh and a cough.

"Finish your beers and come with me. I have some excellent tequila. My cousin owns a small factory, and their resposado has no match."

Lopez scooped up his case from under the table and stood to leave. "I am sorry if I offended your heritage," he said.

"At least you didn't say anything about hockey."

"Que?"

"Never mind."

I downed the last Pacifico in a long chug. I motioned to put money on the table. He waved me off.

"It is taken care of."

I followed Lopez out of the bar to the strains of a singer whose song had somehow become even sadder.

* * *

WE ARRIVED AFTER A SHORT DRIVE in Lopez's vintage VW Bug, which was the color of rust and darker rust. Rattling down one of Sayulita's corduroy dirt roads was a good body massage but didn't lessen the tension coursing through me. I'd always had this ability to sense when something was going bad, even when I was a kid. Once during a pick-up baseball game I'd felt a twinge. Two full minutes later, the thick-as-a-brick eleven-year-old batter spun his Louisville and smacked the kid on deck square on the chops, eliciting a fountain of blood and a collective moan from the bench. I wasn't even surprised when it happened. I knew it was coming.

Now, walking into a low-slung structure overgrown with Mexican foliage, I knew I wasn't going into any kid's ballgame. I also knew I wasn't going anywhere good.

Inside was less shabby than the outside. Light poured in the open windows, and plants from the front yard had migrated and taken root in pots around the large square living space, their rich greens a stark contrast with the buttermilk walls. A blue curtain hung from a golden rod, sealing off a hallway that led somewhere I didn't want to know. And then there was the scuzzy guy on the wicker easy chair smoking the stub of a cigar, the ring of smoke around him looking less like a halo and more like a swarm of bees. There was only a couple inches left, but I made out the red band of a Romeo y Julieta, most likely courtesy of Lopez. Or possibly, scuzzy-guy was the supplier to the whole show. The dude looked like an extra from a John Huston desert movie.

"Who's this?" He growled his question around and through the smoke.

"Let's start with who the fuck are you?" I asked.

Scuzzy scratched his beard, took a long drag, and blew out a cloud. "Who is he, Lopez?"

"From the north."

"California?"

Lopez smiled his bushy smile. "Farther."

Scuzzy considered this, and I waited until a ten-watt light went off in his head.

"Oh. Canadian. All right, then. Let's talk business or drink."

"How about both?" I asked.

"So it's true what they say about your kind?" Scuzzy asked.

"Every bit of it."

The two men exchanged looks, and I swear I heard Lopez's eyebrows lift—even though I had no fucking clue what they were referring to.

The man on the wicker chair took a final drag before crushing the cigar in a nearby plant. There was a sound like sneakers on a basketball court, and over to my left a bright green gecko high-tailed it up the wall.

"Esmerelda." Scuzzy barked the name like it was a magic spell.

The woman from the beach bar emerged through the blue curtain that matched her intense eyes.

"Didn't expect to see you here," I lied.

"Do I know you?"

Her accent was definitely Latin, but somewhere farther south, I guessed. I'd met an acquaintance of Benno's from Brazil, and there was something similar in her tone.

"In the palapa," I said.

A few moments.

"Where?"

"With the guitar player. You had a shaker."

"Oh." She glanced at Scuzzy. "You're interested in a purchase?"

"Is that what you call it?"

Another glance.

"If you are already here, don't waste our time," she said. "No games."

"Lopez brought me. Can't say I know why."

"You are looking for an," she paused, "arrangement?"

Another sneaker sound from the wall, either the same gecko or another one searching for the same bugs.

"Maybe you can help me. I'm looking for a young woman named Soleil. She could go by the name Sunny." I fished my wallet out and held up the small photo Morales had given me. "Maybe you want to pass this around?"

The room got way too quiet. I thought I heard a gecko tongue a bug.

"I do not think you are who you say you are." Esmeralda spoke in a low tone matching the atmosphere that hung over the room.

"I didn't say I was anybody." I put the picture back.

Scuzzy let out a cracked whistle. Esmeralda looked behind her, and we all watched the guitar player come through the curtain, weathered instrument in hand.

"Oh, good. The band is here," I said.

"Where did you find him, Lopez?" Scuzzy got out of the wicker and took a step toward me.

"He was in Las Sirenas. I thought that he— "

"Carlos!"

Everything moved two or three beats too fast. Esmeralda sprang up and took a fast step back. Carlos the guitar player swung for my head. I ducked, narrowly missing a face full of acoustic wood. When I spun out of the crouch, Scuzzy charged like a hairy rhino and slammed into me. Knocked on my ass and gasping for breath, I held up a hand.

"Hang on, I— "

Scuzzy cut my sentence short with a sharp kick in the ribs.

"I am sorry. I did not suspect, Marco. How did you know?" Lopez looked confused.

"I always know."

"Marco," Guitar-Carlos began. "Who is this?"

"What should we do?" Esmerelda asked. "Perhaps he is with the law."

"Shh. He is with no one."

Lopez raised his hand.

"Shut up, Lopez. Let me think."

So Scuzzy had a name too, and it seemed he was in charge. Pain radiated across my ribcage, and I knew I needed to put something together damn fast. The next boot was probably going to be in my head, followed by something pointy or something that fired bullets. The four of them started talking fast in Spanish. I couldn't follow it, but I guessed I presented them with a problem. I didn't know who they thought I was, but I was pretty sure they were discussing where to dig the hole for my body.

As good a time as any.

I swung out a foot and caught Marco, who I still preferred calling Scuzzy, at the back of his leg. He cried out, grabbed his calf, and fell to one knee. A quick step up, my weight on my back leg, and I slammed him with a hard right, followed by an uppercut to his chin hard enough to make the geckos stop mid-squeak. I turned to Lopez, who was fishing in his jacket. I didn't want to know what it was, so I slammed him in the gut. He let out a whoof, and then I finished with a haymaker that would have made my boxing coach in Montreal proud.

"Amigo!"

I took a fast step behind the timbering Lopez, surprised that Carlos had announced his presence as he came at me. Another swing of his guitar, and this one made contact, clipping the side of my head. It stung like hell, but I grabbed the neck and wrenched it out his hand.

"Hope you've got a backup."

I whipped the guitar around and clocked Carlos on the side of his head. The wood split on contact, and the strings rang out with a jazz chord. Sounded like a diminished ninth, but how the fuck did I know? Carlos joined Lopez on the floor. Surprisingly, Scuzzy was up again. He was rewarded with a boot to the noggin and sent to the darkness.

"I guess it's just you and me." I took in a breath. My chest was sore, and my head burned, but it didn't seem like anything was broken.

The woman with the striking blue eyes kicked off her sandals, crouched down, then started a slow spin, shifting her body from side to side. She planted her hands on the floor and flipped her body backward, scraping the ceiling with her feet.

"Oh, I see. Like that," I said.

"Do you know Capoeira?"

"Jazz drummer from the fifties?"

"I am from Brazil. In my country, peasants learned to fight this way to disguise their training from their oppressors."

"I would think those kind of moves might look a bit suspicious."

Esmeralda was airborne, her feet pointed toward me. For about half a second it was really something to watch. It's an odd thing getting kicked in the head and thinking, hmm, she has really smooth skin.

When I came to, she stood over me, one of those tender tootsies poised over my head. Even in my dazed condition, I was impressed with her balance.

"Why did you come here?"

"Morales." I said the name with too many s's.

"Who is that?" she asked with a small tremor in the foot.

Scuzzy groaned. He was a tough son of a bitch for a cigar smoker. Turning my neck, I saw he was up on his knees. Carlos was also sitting up. A long line of blood trailed down his forehead onto his flowery shirt. Lopez was still down. I spied a chunk of black in his hand. It was whatever he'd been reaching for.

"I said—"

I grabbed her foot and twisted hard before she could drive it down. We were a pair of circus performers. As my move corkscrewed her, she hit the floor with her palms and was ready to spring again. I was a hairpin quicker and kicked her hard in the ass. It wasn't pretty, and I wasn't proud. I wasn't Brazilian.

I slid across the floor and grabbed the gun out of Lopez's hand. I fired one into the ceiling and one into Carlos's split guitar.

"Hey, I need that."

"Learn the flute," I said.

"That makes no sense."

"Shut up. I've had enough of all of you." I fired again into the ceiling. There was a splat next to me as a headless gecko hit the floor. *Shit.*

"You are a cruel man," Esmerelda said.

I had a couple of seconds of regret for the dead lizard, but under the circumstances I moved out of my emotional state damn fast. The gunshots had brought Lopez out of his hibernation.

"You, Scuzzy, uh, Marco, go over and sit by him." I pointed the gun toward the bleeding guitar player. "You too, Lopez."

"What? Who are you?" Lopez was still stunned.

"Doesn't matter. Get over there. Esmerelda too, make a nice tight group like you're on a camp sleepover."

"You are a—"

"Canadian." I cut her off. "And all that weird shit you heard is true."

I didn't have a lot of bravado left in me, so I needed to finish this up.

"If you are going to execute us, do it quickly," Marco said. "But know that our deaths will not go unanswered."

"Where is Soleil?" I asked.

"Who?" Lopez asked.

"We don't know anyone with that name," Esmerelda added.

"Sunny, then. Or some other form of it. Maybe just Sol?"

Nothing from the fun bunch.

"So why did you all turn on me?" I asked.

"You had a look about you," Marco said.

"We have learned that when the undercover ones come, they are usually asking for someone. We believed you were that," Esmerelda said.

I looked down at the dead gecko. Dammit, even the innocent get hurt.

"Here's what's going to happen," I started.

CHAPTER SEVEN

I'D PUSHED THE GROUP behind the curtain, half-expecting to find others back there, maybe the ones they were offering for purchase. My body tensed. But there was only a small table and another door that led to a baño. I told them all to stay there for an hour, and if I caught any of them following me, I'd shoot out their kneecaps. It sounded sufficiently badass, though I'd never do something like that. They didn't need to know that.

Now, I stepped into the Sayulita heat. I didn't think the small leaf-covered house was that much cooler until I got outside. I had absolutely nothing to show for my time in there except for the goose egg on the side of my head. I touched it, almost surprised there was no blood. But I never was a bleeder. The trainer at the boxing club in Montreal always liked that about me.

"Damn, Fischer. Don't you ever bleed?"

"It's too messy," I'd told him.

I also decided to keep Lopez's gun. It was a Colt 1911, something I'd fired before. I also made him give me the nifty black shoulder holster he was sporting. He complained, and I smacked him in the head to make my point. I put the Colt in the holster and pulled my shirt over my khakis.

I made my way down a road I guessed took me back to the way I'd come in, as close to a city center as Sayulita had. I'd paid attention to the side streets Lopez had driven to get here in case I had to make a quick exit. I hadn't figured on getting into a brawl with some human traffickers or shooting a gecko. I still felt bad about that. Little guy was minding his own business and then blam, he lost his head. That seems to be the way it goes in life.

I went past a couple of taco joints that had seen better days and a lot more customers. A shop owner sat in an orange plastic chair and had a smoke. He gave a half-hearted hand wave to call me into his store, which looked like mostly t-shirts and bongs, but his heart wasn't in it. I strode past, refusing to look behind to see if any of them had followed.

So was that what they were, traffickers? The word had popped into my head. I knew it happened, surely all around the world, but I'd never come across it first-hand. Esmerelda had asked if I wanted to make a purchase, but then Lopez said something about not being pigs. I still had no idea what triggered them to think I was someone to be worried about. Something in the accent I had, but never heard, maybe tipped them off. We folks from the great white north have this habit of pronouncing every syllable. Or so I'd been told.

I couldn't really call this progress in looking for Morales's daughter. None of them seemed to recognize the name or the picture. Still, there was a burning in my gut that didn't come from the hot salsa or lack of beer, though I made a note to remedy that. If I were a detective like in one of those books, I'd track down some random clue and put it all together. Yep. Definitely needed a beer.

The number of people on the street increased as the shops got a bit cleaner and the wares shinier. There were floral shirts hanging off hooks next to rows of sandals in every color of the rainbow. Hell, they even had a couple of brown pairs. Now the owners were talking to me in English and Spanish, calling me to come in and buy a shirt, some shoes, toys for my kids, tequila, weed, and they had some plastic lizards that reminded me of my dead ceiling friend.

What made people reach a point in their life where they need to sell another person? Sure, there was the usual greed, corruption, addiction, and abject poverty. That would make you do some bad shit. Maybe that's all it was. What else did you need to be brought to awareness of the fragility of your own life? If you're in the gutter and you can't see a way out, you might be brought to that.

Shit. That gave these bastards too much credit. A darkness crept into my consciousness, not a single thought, but just a cloud of oppression and pain. If that's what happened to Morales's daughter, then what could I do about it? She was bought, sold, abused, and things I didn't want to think about. The darkness lodged in me and held no answers.

I recognized a shop from the street I'd walked in on. Across from me, a surfer carried a blood-red board. He wore a sleeveless shirt exposing full sleeves of tattoos on both shoulders that ran down his tightly muscled biceps and forearms. As I got closer, I saw that the tattoos were of orange fish, maybe koi, swimming through reeds. It was beautiful work, and I wanted to stop him and say that. My attention was grabbed when a loud voice yelled in Spanish. I spun around to see a kid pushing another one in the street. It was the kid on the bike that took my money. He wasn't the one yelling. It was the other taller and broader kid who had him by his Thriller shirt.

"Hey," I called over.

The two ignored me. The big one wound up and clocked the Thriller kid, no longer on his bike. He drew back a leg to punctuate the punch with a boot to the head. I ran into the street. I shouted again.

"Alto. Alto!"

The kicker turned back to see who was making so much noise. Little bugger put his hands on his hips and planted himself in a what-the-fuck-do-you-want stance. While we were having our gunfighters-in-the-street showdown, with me trying to figure out what to do next, the Thriller kid wound up and nailed the big kid with a punch right to the kidneys. Damn, I felt that one. The kid yelped and spun around, but his assailant was already hightailing it down the street.

The big kid said something in Spanish to me and then started to cry.

"Yeah, those hurt like hell," I said. "Go home and have your mom put a hot compress on it, you know like a cloth soaked in hot water."

"Que?"

I wanted to give the kid a hug, but I wasn't there to do juvenile counseling. Plus, he looked like the one that had started it.

"You'll be okay."

I put my hand on his shoulder and then continued down the street. Chances are the two of them would be at it again later today, or maybe they were best buds. Never can tell with these things. The altercation had at least directed my thoughts away from where they were headed.

A row of tented stalls ran off to the left of me where a road dipped down. The first stall held a number of brightly colored pots but no vendor around, just an empty wooden chair. The next had racks of patterned fabrics, deep oranges, blues, and golds hung next to cream-colored cloths with delicate embroidery. A slight breeze had risen and wafted through the stall, making the cloths dance and shimmer.

"Buenas tardes."

She was a young woman, I could almost say a girl, with a smile as warm as her wares. Her stall smelled of cloves and ocean air.

"These are really beautiful. What do people do with them?"

"They have many uses. Some cover tables, or chairs, or wraps," she said.

"Wraps?"

She laughed, a sound as gentle as the wind. "In the evening after the sun goes down. One can wrap them around their shoulders for warmth. Is it cold where you are from?"

"It can be."

"Then perhaps something for your wife." She tilted her head. "Or, I'm sorry, I don't want to assume."

It was my turn to laugh. When I saw the redness in her cheeks, I cut it short.

"Who makes these? Do you?"

"Oh, no. I just run this shop for my mother. There are many excellent Zapotec weavers in Sayulita and in the surrounding areas. We pay them a fair wage for their work."

She wore a bright white shirt tucked into a navy dress with white embroidered flowers across the waistband and down one of the sides.

"Your dress was made by one of these, um, artists?"

"Yes. You have a good eye. And artists is a good word."

"What was the 'Z' word you used?"

"Zapotec. Part of our wonderful culture. Are you here on vacation, señor?"

"Of a kind. Can I ask you something?"

"Of course. About the weavings?"

"Not really." I lifted my hand like it could rain. "This little shop, or tent, or stall … you can make enough money doing this? To live, I mean?"

The young woman's mouth drew a straight line.

"Sorry. I don't mean to offend you. I'm just trying to understand something," I said.

"If you are here to proposition me, then I would ask you to leave my place of business immediately." She squeezed one of her hands into a tight fist, and the knuckles whitened.

I still had my hand up in the air like an idiot, so I slowly brought it down, palm up. I put my other hand in the same position, hoping for vulnerability. The gesture seemed forced, and in her face I saw she knew it.

"I would never do anything like that. Again, I apologize," I said.

"Then why do you ask this?"

"I'm truly curious how people make a living here. You said this is your mother's shop. Does your father also work?"

"He is dead. For more than ten years."

She brought up her closed fist and then crossed her arms. Her expression was unchanged, maybe even harder. I held my stance and lowered my eyes.

"Perhaps in your country," she started before barking out a cough, "perhaps in your country this is a usual question. We are more private about these matters."

"I know. I've lived here for a while."

Her eyes widened, and she did the tilted head thing again. "In Sayulita? I have never seen you before, and it is not a big place. I would know."

"More in P.V. And also a small place on the ocean, south, Melaque."

"I know of it. Where the pelicans fish in the bay," she said.

"It's a lovely place."

"Why are you here in Sayulita?"

"I'm looking for someone."

"Someone like who? You are not being clear, and I'm going to ask that you leave again."

"I was hired to find a man's relative. His daughter."

She turned her gaze to the dirt floor, but only for a moment. I wasn't sure, but I thought the tension in her body might have softened.

"I'm assuming this young woman is in peril? Or is she a child?"

"Your English is very good."

"What do you mean you were hired? Are you policía? An investigator of some kind?"

"Not really. Or not at all," I said.

She unfolded her arms, coughed again, then rubbed her hands together like she needed to wash something off.

"Do you have a cold or allergy?"

"Are you here to purchase something or to only ask these questions?"

I sighed. "I'm not going to keep apologizing, señorita... What is your name?"

"It is of no significance."

"Fair enough." I paused.

In another moment, I was going have to leave. I didn't want to bother her. But I was curious. Working here, she would meet a lot of people, turistas and locales. She was someone who probably knew a lot of people. It was a long shot, but lately I had nothing else.

"Listen. I'm sorry, and that's the last one you get. I'm not trying to be rude, and I'm not trying to get something from you."

"What are you trying?"

"It's been a helluva day. I came from a place where they are holding women against their will. Making them do things that no one should be forced to do. I'm trying to do something about it."

"Did you see this?"

"No. But I know it."

She rubbed her eyes. "They are trafficking," she said.

"You know the term?"

"Of course I do. I am not stupid. I know this happens in our country and right here in our city." She pointed at me. "You say you are trying, but it is because of men like you."

"Like me?"

She stiffened. "They are driven by desires women do not know of, or perhaps of a different kind. Some men know how to control this. Still, it hides beneath. I believe the word is lurks. And when this desire emerges, it twists, and people suffer. And by people, I mean women. Young women. Children."

"Yes. I am sorry. I know this. It's very bad," I said.

"It is evil, señor."

"Fischer. My name is Fischer. And I agree with you."

I extended my hand. She looked at it but did not move. We stood in the stall. The only sound was the breeze ruffling the fabrics. Finally, I moved to leave.

"Señor."

"Yeah?"

"If you knew my family, you would understand my emotion. I am this way because of—" She stopped.

"It's okay. I don't need to understand. I wish you all the best in your business and your life."

Two small children ran down the street squealing. Both carried long red ribbons tied to sticks.

"You said that you are not policía, but perhaps you are with one of the organizations, like the FBI. Is this true?"

"I'm from Canada. We don't have that. Like I said, I was hired to find someone. Why are you asking me this?"

"My sister. She—" Her voice caught, and she swallowed. "I am sorry."

"She was taken?"

"Or she went willingly. We are not sure. She followed a dark path for some time. I saw this more than anyone else. Drugs were involved, and the type of people that engage in those activities." She wiped her eyes and straightened. "I know of a group that is involved. I have wanted to confront them, but my mother has forbidden me to go there. She is worried what would happen."

"Where is this group?"

"Bucerias. Not very far south. Do you know it?"

"I came through there, yeah."

A couple of turistas entered the stall, and the young woman excused herself to talk with them. They fingered the hanging fabric. The man barely seemed interested. The woman was clad in neon yellow and orange that really didn't go together, clothing that was an offence next to the beautiful weavings that filled the tented stall. She talked too fast and with an edge in her voice. The man gave an out-of-tune whistle. I didn't hear everything, but I knew they were haggling for a price. This Mexican stereotype had so pervaded the minds of turistas that they believed absolutely everything was up for negotiation. The couple had no idea, or ignored, the incredible amount of hours that went into this kind of work.

It took a lot of self-restraint not to walk over, smack him right in his whistler, and tell them both to get the fuck out.

They left without buying anything or thanking the owner for her time.

"You get a lot like those?" I asked.

"Certain times of year, yes."

"They lack basic respect."

"It is of no matter."

"Tell me more about this group from Bucerias."

She didn't respond right away, looking out to the street as the same pair of children from before raced by. "I have some horchata in a cooler. Would you like some?"

"I would."

She pulled a blue chest from below one of the tables and took out a glass jar full of a milky liquid. I'd had the drink before. Though it was sweeter than my usual taste, it had an icy freshness that I welcomed.

"Lucia."

"Sorry?"

"My name is Lucia. You asked earlier. And my sister is Celestina."

She poured herself a glass of horchata, and as we drank together, she laid out the story of her troubled sister. I'd heard ones like it before. Minor rebellion caused by puberty and a need by the parents, or in this case her mother, to shut down and control their child. As usual, the kid kicked against the bricks and then fell in with the wrong people. Hidden sips of wine turned into tequila and then into weed, and soon cocaine showed up, most often in the form of crack.

"When was the last time you saw her?"

"Two weeks ago, she was at the terminal."

"The bus station?"

"Si. La estación. I thought she had only then arrived in Sayulita, but she said she'd been back a while and now had to leave again. Her eyes did not look correct."

"How do you mean?"

"They were not focused, always moving. I am guessing it was because of the drugs. She was glad to see me and gave me a long hug before a man came along, tapped her on the shoulder, and she followed him onto the bus."

"Where was the bus headed?"

"South. San Ignacio, Las Parotas, Bucerias."

"You said you knew of a group down there. How?" I asked.

"After my sister left, I spoke with a group of young men at the terminal. They didn't want to tell me anything, but I recognized one whose mother I knew. I told him I would tell his mother what he was involved in with these other boys. Because that's really what they were. Boys, not men."

"What was the kid you threatened involved in?"

She laughed. "I have no idea. I said it only to scare him."

It was good to see her shoulders relax, but the smile was gone right away.

"They told me that Celestina had been working here in Sayulita. She was brought here by the man on the bus and two others."

"Working at what?"

Lucia put her hands in her lap and studied them. "You know what, señor."

It was another minute before she spoke again. The shadow of the tent had shrunk, and the sun crept closer to us as we talked.

"Will you go and find my sister? Talk to her, tell her that things are different at home now. Mama wants to see her very badly. Tell her we can help her. Tell her…" Lucia began to weep.

"I can't promise anything. I'll see what I can do."

"Thank you, señor Fischer. That is an unusual name. Is it common where you are from in Canada?"

"You can call me Luke."

"Ah. Almost like my name." She paused. "I believe it is a sign that we met. Perhaps this will lead you to the one you seek. As well as Celestina. This is often how these things happen. If we hold on to hope."

"That's a big if, Lucia. Did the boy at the terminal say much more … like, where in Bucerias?"

"He only said that the men also owned horses. And that they took them for walks along the beach."

"That's not much."

"It is all I know. Bucerias is not a large place. If you ask the right questions, I am sure a man like you will find something."

"A man like me?"

"Yes."

I stood in silence, waiting for more, but Lucia offered nothing else.

As I moved to leave the stall, she wiped her eyes and extended her hand to me. When I took it, she brought me into an embrace. She smelled of cinnamon and something floral.

We exchanged no more words. I left the tent and squinted into the bright afternoon sun. I thought I knew where the terminal was, but with the crazy layout of Sayulita roads, I couldn't be sure. I wasn't sure of a lot of things.

CHAPTER EIGHT

I'D NEVER TRIED TO UNDERSTAND why I have the worst sense of direction. I've always been that way. Spin me around in a room and I might have a hard time finding the door. So when I couldn't find the right road to the bus station, I wasn't all that surprised, just pissed off. I walked under a row of parota trees that gave some reprieve from the sun sending arrows of heat down on my head. They had those leaves that had me imagining being fanned with them as I ate grapes, or at least tacos.

A guy around my age wearing a sparkling white shirt passed me, and I stopped him.

"Sorry. I don't speak much Spanish. I'm looking for the terminal. Can you direct me there. Donde terminal?"

"La estación?"

I recognized the word Lucia had used.

"Yes. Estacion. Si."

I said my words like a Spanish Tarzan. Me Luke. The guy looked me up and down, surveying this sweaty turista and likely trying to gauge if he should help me.

"Come with me, señor, I'll take you there." He beckoned me with a curved finger.

"Mucho apreciado."

He grunted and walked quickly ahead of me. I almost had to jog to catch up. He looked back, again with the finger-move, and then pointed to a skinny road that ran between two buildings. I knew I hadn't come that way before.

"I don't think it's that way."

"Fast cut," he said.

"Short cut?"

"Si. Ven por aquí."

I was tired and hot, recently having a guitar swung at my head, complete with goose egg on my noggin, and I'd had an emotional talk with a young women vendor. These are the things I told myself when I followed the man in white into what was basically a Mexican alleyway. He turned slowly and brought out a knife almost as sparkly as his shirt.

"Seriously?" I asked.

This time the finger-beckoning meant he wanted whatever I had.

"Look, buddy. I'm not a turista. I live here. Well, not here, but around here."

"I do not care, señor." He rotated the knife in the air. "Give me all your money or I will put this blade in your stomach."

I sighed. I was completely not in any mood for this shit. I reached deep into my khaki pocket and thought about a move where I could whip out the hidden Colt. Instead, I bent my body like I was trying hard to procure something for him.

"Move more slowly, señor. This is very sharp."

He poked the knife toward me and I tripped forward. He stumbled back, only for a second, just long enough to shoot my hand out and grab his wrist hard. With my free hand, I popped him hard. My fist smashed into his nose, eliciting a fresh spurt of blood. My knee came up into his crotch and drove home my point. He let out an oof that could have been in Spanish. It didn't matter at this point. He'd dropped the knife, and I heaved it far down the alley, hoping I didn't spear a strolling cat.

"Lo siento. I don't have time for this." I was proud I'd remembered the word.

Now he was the one bent over. Mumbling something, he spat a white stream on the ground.

"Yeah, well pick a better mark next time."

He flinched and shot his arm out. I decided to close up our business with a haymaker to the chin. I don't think I broke his jaw, but it would hurt like hell when he woke up. I didn't make it a habit of street fighting, but I had shit to do.

Stepping back on the street, I moved quickly away from the alley. The pain in my head had lessened, probably from the adrenalin. I strode in a random but hopeful direction. An old man smoked a cigar, perched on a concrete step outside a tobacco shop.

"Buenes tardes," I said.

He nodded gave a wink and a finger pistol. I wasn't sure if he'd heard anything of what happened in the alley or he was just being friendly.

I pointed ahead of me. "Terminal?"

He nodded. "Si." He brought his hand out to gesture in the direction I was walking and then curved it right.

"Gracias."

I was given another wink and a broad smile. The old guy must have seen that I was covered in a layer of sweat after my tussle with the street thief. I wondered how a guy like that kept his shirt so white. Maybe that was part of his schtick. No one assumes the guy in the sharp shirt also carried a sharp knife. I gave my sore-again head a shake, reminding myself to be more aware.

The cobblestone street started to fill with people. Not sure where everyone had gone while I was busy trying not to get stabbed. Mexico was like this somehow, or my experience of it anyway. People ebbed and flowed like the nearby surf. I'd be wading through a crowd jostling for position or trying to avoid kids barrel-assing on bikes and then find myself on a street where it was me and a couple of skinny cats. I realized I hadn't seen any cats or other animals in town. Could be they were scared off by the surfers. Like they'd been listening to my thoughts, two cats bounded past, one chasing the other, flashing a memory of the boys whose fight I'd interrupted.

There were times when I related, too much really, to the felines chasing each other. It wouldn't be long before one of them spun around and started after the other, giving their version of the kidney-punch thrown by the kid in the Thriller shirt. I was poking into something that had the high probability of turning on me. Getting a guitar in the head or avoiding a mugger's blade were minor consequences compared with what might be waiting for me.

Ahead, I saw the tall concrete wall painted the color of Meyer lemons. *Terminal de Autobuses* was emblazoned in thick black letters. Behind the station a hill rose, half covered in foliage, with orange-roofed buildings poking their heads up like school children. The sky was painted the perfect bluc, a light breeze cooled my sweaty neck, and the events of the last couple of hours faded with the distant cries of gulls.

CHAPTER NINE

I KNEW MY PRONUNCIATION SUCKED, and sure, it bugged me, but not so much that I'd be forced to take Spanish lessons. I'd asked the man at the counter, a thin sort with a thick mane of hair that didn't fit on his head, when the next bus left for Bucerias. He had no idea what place I meant until I'd said it three times and he finally said back to me, "Bucerias?"

I was pretty damn sure one of my attempts had hit three out of four of those syllables.

"Yes, si. What the hell did you think?"

A flop of that swampy hair fell over his brow. He must have thought that was his grumpy look. It seemed well-practiced. I swallowed my smart-ass remark, muttered "lo siento," paid for my ticket, and went to wait with the others on the chunk of concrete that stood in for a bus platform.

My time in Sayulita was brief, only a few hours. But from watching the surfers to drinking Pacificos to almost getting my lights punched out by Scuzzy, or crowned by the guitar player and his Brazilian martial arts partner, well, I was ready to get the fuck out of Dodge. I had less than zero interest in returning.

The segunda was a nice one, lush seats, and damned if it didn't have A.C. We were about half-full, and I thought the driver would wait for more riders, but he suddenly lurched out of the station.

I needed to pay more attention to the signs this time, or I'd miss Bucerias again, end up in P.V., and have to start over like the worst kid's board game. On the other hand, I could just go to the Rosita, say the hell with it, and order a table full of Pacificos. The idea was more than a little appealing.

Morales ... what did I owe him? Nothing. But I owed Benno a lot. He kept me in work, paid my hotel tab, and kind of looked over me. Morales told me he was friends with Benno, or an associate or something. For the time being I was honoring this, until I found out different. It was unclear how long he'd be out of the country.

Benno wasn't a father figure, unless organized criminals could be called that. The Italians had the "dons," or so the movies made me believe. The only Don I'd ever met was a guy who fixed cars in my hometown and had that name stenciled on his greasy overalls. Benno didn't seem like one of those mob bosses. For sure not to me. Since I'd known him, I'd come to learn his reach was wide and his power was respected far beyond the city limits of PV.

When I'd first arrived in Mexico, I ended up in one of his main places. Unknown to me at the time, he had an office in the back room. The bar was called Solar or Sunada or something. I no longer remembered because even in the span I'd lived in P.V., it had changed names several times. I now knew it as Benno's. It had a perfect view of the ocean, and Pacificos were ice-cold and the camarones laced with freshest garlic. One night, when I was the last person in the place, Benno approached me.

"Buenas noches, señor. It seems it is just the two of us here ¿hablas español?"

"Spanish? No, sorry."

"Ah. Lo siento."

His voice was low and smooth, like he lived on late-night FM. He saw my confused look.

"Lo siento is sorry in my country. I am glad to meet you, mucho gusto. Let us talk in English. I am very comfortable with it."

"Talk about what?"

"I have noticed you in here this past week. You are always alone."

Something pinched the back of my neck, but I ignored it.

"I like being alone."

"Have you been in our city long? Is this your first time?"

"I'm going to just finish this and leave."

I reached for my now favorite beer, Pacifico, and he put his hand on mine.

"Listen, I don't want to—"

"Disculpe." He patted my hand. "Do not get the wrong idea. I am a very good judge of character. I will buy you another cerveza, or something else if you'd like. It's a quiet evening, and I would like to talk."

"Yeah. So you said."

He got up from the bar and walked down to where the last of the staff was cleaning glasses. He said something to him I couldn't hear, though in Spanish I wouldn't understand it anyway. He came back with a beer and a highball for himself.

"I call this a J and C," he said. "I have a fondness for Jamaican rum."

"Where I come from, rum and Coke is damn near a national beverage."

"And where is that, my friend?"

Our conversation slid into an ease that surprised me. He was right; I'd been on my own a lot, including all the hours of driving across the U.S. and northern Mex.

"There are many people from your country who enjoy vacations here."

He smiled. "My name is Benno."

"Good to meet you. I'm Luke Fischer. Is this your place?"

"Yes. One of them. Are you on a vacation?"

"No. I'd need a job to have one of those."

"Ah. Then you will be with us for a while?"

"Looks like it."

Benno eventually got to it after another beer for me and more rum for him. He wanted me to do some work for him, and he would pay me handsomely for it.

"Do people still say that?" I asked.

"I don't understand," Benno said.

"Handsomely. Seems like an old-timey word, like malarky."

"I don't know that word. You are not interested then?"

"I didn't say that."

Looking back, I didn't know how fortuitous a meeting that first one was. Benno told me he made a lot of land deals. I didn't say anything, or ask for details, but I wouldn't be surprised if drugs were involved; they almost always were. Benno must have gauged my suspicion. He told me he didn't want me to have an inside window to his business. He called it a business, but I knew he meant the back room in that metaphorical way. All kinds of shit goes down in back rooms, and little of it is legal. He wanted me to work as his associate.

"Sounds formal. Is this Mexico's form of Wall Street?"

"Luke, it is better this way. Simply do some work for me when I ask. I will always pay you well."

"Who do you need me to hit?" I'd asked.

"Hit? Like…" He held up a finger pistol. "This is something you are capable of?"

"Uh, no. I won't do that, Benno. I meant punch. Like in boxing, without the ring."

Benno laughed long and hard. There was a warmth in his laughter. It echoed off the walls of his small but very neat office we had retreated to. He took a bottle full of amber liquid from a cabinet and poured us two healthy tumblers.

"Yes, Luke. I may ask you to look over some people, make sure they do not step out of their line. That is how you say it?"

"Sure," I said. "Just watch them?"

"If need be, your strength and yes, your fighting skill will be useful."

"I always like to be useful."

As things turned out, I did have to knock some heads for Benno and disarm guys with knives and the odd gun. I learned I was really good at it. I had fast reflexes from my time in the boxing ring in Montreal and I guess all the fighting I did growing up. I usually only had to throw a punch or two to end things, but there was the one bozo who took a knife in the stomach. It was either that or it was going in my neck. Benno called some people to take him to the hospital. Or somewhere.

Though I was on the periphery of Benno's work, I put together what he did. More importantly to me, I knew what he didn't do. Children were never involved, not even the teens that got pulled into local gangs. They'd steal and break into places, and the money would make its way up to a guy like Benno. When Benno found out that was where the money came from, he severed connections and told those people to do better.

Benno believed in family—could even say that he held it sacred, though he didn't strike me as a churchgoer. He never crossed himself, not even as a joke. Some guys did that after they gave someone a shit-kicking. There's a guy on the floor moaning and bleeding out, and the asshole responsible crossed himself, spat, and let out a fat hippo laugh. I'd seen it more than once. I didn't know if they were being badass or if there was still a small part of them that remembered sitting next to their mom in the pew. Then they'd give a last kick. Sorry, Mom.

Benno also had a lot of respect for women. I knew he wasn't involved in prostitution, or at least I never saw it. For sure nothing like human trafficking. He always treated women very well, whether it was in his office, on the street, or anywhere. If he overheard someone on the street, or even his own man, say something dirty or sexual to a woman, he chided them. They immediately apologized to Benno, and the woman, because they weren't idiots.

A couple in the seat ahead of me started talking fast, and their volume increased. I didn't understand what they were saying, but I didn't have to know Spanish to know they were fighting. She poked a finger into the guy's chest and then did it again with more force. The guy flinched and raised his hand. I wasn't about to break up a domestic squabble, but I was not about to let him hit her.

I coughed loudly, and the man whipped around to face me. His eyes flashed, and there was a line of spit on his bottom lip. I figured in about half a second he was going to come over the seat at me. This was turning into one helluva Thursday. Or was it Monday?

He said something to me through gritted teeth. The woman put a hand on his shoulder, and he flinched like he had when she was poking his chest. The bus lurched to a sudden stop, and the man fell back. The woman shot out her hands and prevented him from falling right out of his seat. She sent a torrent of words at me. I recognized the curses, especially pendejo, which was used multiple times.

I spied a faded green sign that read *Bucerias*. I leapt out of my seat, not waiting to be called a dipshit again, then jammed my hand in the half-closed bus doors. The driver shouted at me.

"Eres un pendejo!"

"Yeah, yeah. So I've been told. Let me off the fucking bus."

Another stream of invectives. It sounded like most of the bus joined in. The doors opened, and I stumbled onto the street. The bus took off in a cloud of burning oil. *Making friends wherever you go, Fischer.*

CHAPTER TEN

BUCERIAS WAS BIGGER than Sayulita, but it didn't have the roads going off in every direction. Still, I had a helluva time finding the beach. High-rises and concrete structures in various stages of construction and demolition lined the highway on the drive into town. That was probably why I missed the sign the first time. Might have been a time when Bucerias was sleepy, but that time had passed.

When in doubt, head west was my motto I'd just come up with. I was fairly certain that was left. The streets were cobbled, like in P.V., in better shape than the Sayulita roads. I walked along a line of shabby low buildings, shops with fabrics and other wares, and then past a taco shop, the air filled with the smell of fried meat and onions. I looked for a break between the buildings and finally came across a grid of concrete squares leading to an arch held up by a pair of green pillars. Painted on the arch in fat letters it read *Acceso A Playa*. It was a good guess this was the beach entry, given that about a hundred yards away the ocean stretched out in a long wavy carpet. Dazzling flecks of light sparkled on the water, the color sliding from deep teal to a gray-blue, and then the cerulean sky dropped down like the most beautiful curtain across the horizon.

To the north, an outcropping of rock cut a jagged edge against the sky. A couple of clay-colored buildings were perched near the top of the rock along with a tall cross, which, given the distance, must have been huge.

Though I'd come looking to talk to people, search for clues and shit, I was actually glad to see the empty water. As I headed south along the beach, the long curved shoreline held a few stragglers that wandered into the surf. Another group of hills were far off where the bay curved in again. The hills sloped and faded in a gray mist while a lazy cloud reached across the thing Neil Young called the blue, blue windows.

"Not bad, Bucerias," I said aloud to no one.

Farther up, tall shapes of hotels or condos poked into the air. Hard to tell which was which, but I knew a number of ex-pats, a lot of Canadians, had bought their little square box of paradise here. A few palapas had sprung up. One looked tonier than the rest, with white tables covered in linen. Blue-striped chairs were tilted at the perfect angle under matching umbrellas. Farther into the restaurant area, white poles opened into patterned bamboo awnings.

The place was called Mary y Sol, and it put the Hotel Rosita's lounge to shame. I sat under a striped umbrella and planned on ordering a big-ass margarita. I knew they were big because I'd spied a waiter carrying one on a tray before I sat down. The view of the ocean from the Mary y Sol was pretty damn spectacular. Sure, I'd walked along the beach to get here, but now I got to sit and contemplate things. I didn't usually go for the salty green cocktails, but I figured these guys knew how to make a good one.

"Anything else, señor?"

The guy's shirt was whiter than the tablecloth, which was a feat in itself. He wore a thin black string tie that looked like it had been ironed before he came on shift—and probably given a fresh press on his breaks.

"Tostado?"

"Of course."

He came back in a few minutes with a frosted thick mug, more of a cauldron, of limey fresh tequila-laced margarita. Throughout the icy drink, the burn of the cactus liquor was perfect. Chunks of rock salt sparkled on the rim. I only took a few sips through the salt, trying to show my liver and general constitution some respect.

While I waited for the food, I watched the surf. A man, likely in his thirties, played with his son at the edge of the water. There were no surfers here, but also no waves worth riding like the ones at Sayulita.

The tostadas came on a beautiful plate with bean dip, a watermelon wedge in a perfect triangle pointed to the sky, and damned if there wasn't a rice starfish. I'd never seen one of those before. My server set down a bowl of fresher-than-fresh salsa dotted with some excellent bright green jalapeños. It was going to be tough to remember why I came to Bucerias.

I whiled away the afternoon with the flavorful plate and one more of the giant margaritas before I switched to Pacificos.

"Of course, señor. I will bring you one."

"Better make it dos. I want to watch the sun go down."

"A good choice, señor."

"My name is Fischer."

The waiter nodded.

"Is there a place I could get a room for the night. Cuarto?"

"Yes, señor Fischer." He pointed to a tall structure just south of the restaurant. "We are in business with El Placedor. They have fine accommodations. Would you like me to talk with them and make arrangements?"

"Sure. That'd be swell. But no rush. The cervezas first. Por favor."

"Of course, señor. Your Spanish is very excellent," he lied.

I liked that he called me by my name right away. I could get used to eating in this kind of establishment, as long as Morales was paying. That reminded me to call him, say where I was, and ask him if he'd gleaned anything else about the Bucerias connection. I trusted that Lucia had told me the truth about where her sister had gone and who had taken her there. I was more inclined to help her than Morales, except he was footing the bill, and it was more than possible I'd never see the woman in the weaving stall again.

The Pacificos slid down my throat like toddlers on a waterslide. The sun was a navel orange turning bloody as it sizzled into the Pacific. A long, low-pitched gull call echoed off the distant hills, and an ancient pelican came in for one last fish before someone turned out the lights.

CHAPTER ELEVEN

EL PLACEDOR HAD THE USUAL open-air lobby. The floor was covered in terra cotta tiles that looked clean enough to eat tacos off of. The server at Mary y Sol had told me to talk to a woman named Carlita, the name I now read on the white badge of a diminutive woman with her dark hair tied in a neat bun.

"I was told you had a room for me."

Her smile lit up the lobby. "Of course. You must be señor Fischer."

"Is it that obvious?"

She gave a puzzled look. "We were told that a señor—"

I stopped her. "It's all good. Nice to be recognized. Do you have a phone I can use?"

"There is the one here." She pointed to the boxy black phone on her counter. "Or if you'd like some privacy, there is one around the corner."

"I'll take the private one."

"Is the call local?"

"P.V."

She hesitated. "To Puerto there will be a charge."

"Add it to the room," I said.

She handed me a room key and a form to sign. I went to call Morales.

"Señor Fischer, I have been waiting to hear from you."

"I know."

"You do?"

"What's going on, Morales? I need some more information. What have you heard since we met?"

Morales coughed into the phone, and I pulled the earpiece away.

"Where are you calling me from?"

"Bucerias."

"You have stayed there since we spoke?"

"Side-trip to Sayulita."

"Ah, good. And what did you find there?"

"How to dodge a swinging guitar. Well, almost."

"I do not understand."

A cleaning lady slid by with a giant cart full of spray bottles, white buckets, and linen.

"Disculpe."

I moved out of her way while she sprayed the mirror on the wall next to me.

"Never mind," I said to Morales. "Whattya got?"

"I have not found out anything—oh, except that Soleil's boyfriend has turned up."

"In P.V.? Or Sayulita. I saw a lot of surfers with leg tattoos."

Morales breathed into the phone before answering. "He is here in the city. But no longer alive."

"No shit?"

More breathing.

"Which place are you at in Bucerias?" Morales asked.

"Toney joint by the name of El Placedor."

"Good. Good. I know this place. I am known there as well, and they can send me the bill."

"Already told them that." The cleaning lady disappeared into a room down the hall. "So the boyfriend is dead. What does that mean, and how did you find that out anyway?"

"I have may connections here, including members of the policía. I left word with a friend that if someone showed up matching the description I gave, they should contact me."

"How did he die?"

"I am not sure of the details. His body was found in the water."

"Drowned, then. Hit a rogue wave."

"Again, I am not certain."

Something in his voice. Ramone was holding back what he knew.

"Listen, Morales. I came here because someone I met in Sayulita said some kind of bad shit was going down here. I don't know what it was or who was doing it."

"I see."

"Maybe you do, maybe you don't. But here I am. Happy to drink margaritas on your tab unless you got something for me to look at."

"Who told you of this shit in Bucerias? And of what kind do you mean?"

"It doesn't matter. I've found out nothing." I didn't feel the need to tell him I'd also done nothing but drink and eat, two of the things I'm best at.

"There is a man who lives near the hotel. He has some information that will be useful in your search for Soleil."

"Who is this guy? And how do you know he knows anything? If you want me to find your daughter, you need to come clean."

"Clean. Yes. I understand." Morales coughed. "You are not the only one I have reached out to, señor Fischer."

"I feel cheap."

A long silence on the phone.

"You speak in a strange manner." Morales coughed again; he must have been trying to set free a couple of throat frogs.

"Where do I find this guy? He going to just arrive on a horse?"

"After we are finished our call, I will contact him, and he will meet you at the hotel. What is your room number?"

I looked at the gold letters on the red leather tag. "Two-one-six."

"Good. Do you need me to wire you some money? I can send it to the hotel."

"Not going to say no to that."

"A horse?"

"Never mind."

"Anything else, señor Fischer?"

A couple came up behind me in the narrow hallway. They were swaying in a way that said they were having a good night.

"Señor, will you be much longer?" the man slurred.

They both looked in their twenties. Youthful little shits probably wouldn't even have a hangover tomorrow. I held up two fingers.

"Un momento," I said, then lowered my voice. "Morales, are you aware of a trafficking ring operating out of Sayulita?"

"Sorry, you are hard to hear. Can you repeat that?"

"You heard me," I said.

"Do you mean the buying and selling of citizens?"

There was a catch in his throat.

"Of women, yeah."

Another long pause. I looked back at the couple, who had decided to engage in some tongue gymnastics while they waited for me.

"Do you think this is what has happened to Soleil? If so, I..." Morales swallowed back a sob. "Perhaps that is why her boyfriend was killed."

"I thought he drowned." I waited for another response, but there was none. "Send me the money, Morales."

I put the phone on the cradle. I wanted to tip my hat to the couple but I remembered I didn't have one. The woman wobbled, her knee about to give out, until her gallant suitor held her back up.

"Gracias. Buenas noches, señor."

"Stay safe, you crazy kids."

The man looked at me with wide eyes, but then the woman giggled and blew in his ear. I left them to it.

I went to the lounge and asked for a margarita to take to my room. I'd heard lime was a good sleeping tonic.

"Heavy on the tequila."

The server gave me a too-deep nod before he handed me the plastic cup.

CHAPTER TWELVE

THE ROOM WAS SIMPLE, but the bed was the right kind of soft, and that was all the mattered. I drew the curtain on the sliding door to a small balcony that looked onto the dark Pacific. I fell asleep to the waves beating a gentle rhythm. I think it was six-eight time, but it could have been a waltz.

I was roused out of a dream where Sam and I were on a long drive on a winding Michigan road. I thought the pounding noise was distant lumberjacks working the afternoon away.

"Dammit. Okay, okay. Just a momento."

I stumbled to the door, undid the useless chain, and was greeted by a fast punch to the face. There was no time for stars or cartoon birds, so I tilted back and then steadied myself.

My door guest drove his fist into my stomach, and I doubled over. The margarita gurgled inside me, but before it could escape, something hard and heavy came down on the back of my head, and I said hello and goodnight to the floor.

* * *

I DON'T THINK I WAS OUT LONG. Blurry shapes came into focus, and I identified two goons, one short and broad, the other tall and broader. I liked it better when they matched. I realized the short one was sitting down, so he could have been closer in size to the other one—except his feet were dangling like a kid having a sandwich and lemonade at the lunch counter.

"You are putting your nose where it doesn't belong, señor?"

"What?"

I was never that articulate after being knocked out. I felt my holster under my shirt and knew it was empty.

"We took it." Shorty read my gesture. "We were sent by someone to talk with you."

"Funny way of talking. Felt more like punching." I gingerly touched the back of my head. There was a large goose egg next to the previous one and some wetness I knew wasn't lemonade.

"We think it would be a good idea for you to check out now and go back to where you came from," the short one said.

I pointed at the tall, so far non-talking, goon.

"Does he share this opinion?"

The tall one's expression stayed the same. I thought of Easter Island.

"Okay. So which one of you talked to Morales?" I asked.

"We know many people by that name."

"This Morales had one of those annoying goatees that you want to yank."

Both gave a blank stare.

"And this one had a daughter named Soleil."

More nothings.

"Look, if you talked to Morales, he must have told you I'm working for him. You were supposed to come give me information or something. Not give me a stomach massage."

"You are a talker who says nothing," the short one said. "We are not here because of this Morales. So shut up. And get out."

Easter Island pointed out the open door.

"Well, you two have been a huge help." I started to get off the floor, clenching my fist on the way up.

"That is far enough."

The tall one took a giant step toward me. I was halfway up and halfway down, teetering. I think Mr. Statue pictured me squished under his shoe.

"How am I supposed to check out from down here?" I reached out my hand. "Give me some help."

Shorty seemed confused by my request. He nodded to Easter Island, who extended one of his oversized mitts. I grasped it, pulled myself up, and drove my knee as hard as I could into his crotch.

"Hey," Shorty yelled.

The statue was tippy and gasping. I clipped him with two fast punches to the side of his head, then attempted to replicate the blow they gave me to the back of my head. I used both hands, clasped together because I'm a pro. Easter Island timbered and took a nap on the floor I'd just got off of.

"Sure, let's talk," I said.

"Listen, señor."

As Shorty talked, he dipped his hand into his jacket. I lunged for him and gave him a hard cuff to the back of his head. Something shot out of his mouth and scuttled onto the floor. I jammed my hand into his jacket, gave him another slap, and brought out a shiny Glock.

"So what should we talk about?"

Shorty pointed over to the floor, where a set of shiny choppers had slid.

"You need to glue those in better, my friend. Run out of Polygrip?"

"Stupid Yankee," he mumbled.

That earned him another cuff.

"Wrong. You must have missed that week in goon school."

Shorty started to say something but clammed up. He pointed again.

"Yeah, yeah. Well, if I want to understand you, I better get them."

I kept the Glock pointed at him as I bent down and retrieved his dentures, trying not to think about what he'd last eaten.

"Gracias." He slid in the teeth with a click.

"When did you last talk to Soleil? Does Morales even know you're here?"

"I don't choose to answer."

"Okay. I choose to put a bullet in each of your kneecaps."

Shorty swallowed, and a bead of sweat appeared between his unruly brows.

"Me and Zig were told to come to the hotel. We were told to get you to leave. That was all."

"Zig?"

Shorty pointed at the still out Tall-Boy, my new name for him now that he was stretched out.

"Told by who?"

He shook his head. I aimed the Glock at his left knee. I knew I wouldn't do it, but I was banking on him not knowing that.

"This will hurt you more than me. Actually, it won't hurt me at all."

I racked the slide on the semiautomatic.

"Un momento, un momento, señor." Shorty held his hands in the air.

"Morales?"

"Yes. This name was mentioned to me. But in another conversation. I did not meet this man. We work for another."

"Does this another guy have a name?"

Shorty looked over to his large partner still stretched out like a carp on the beach.

"If he wakes up, will he give me the name? What was his name, Zip?"

"Zig."

His eyes flitted, looking for an out and finding nothing.

"C'mon, these bullets are getting cold."

"That does not make sense, señor."

"It's been a long fucking day. Name." I pressed the gun onto his knee. I felt the tremor in his leg.

"I cannot give his name. I will give you an address." Shorty spat out the words.

"Not sure that's enough. But I'm a fair guy. It will only cost you one knee. Deal?"

Zig groaned and stirred. Shorty closed his eyes like there was too much sun in the room.

"He is at the Hotel Palomar."

"Where?"

"Right here in Bucerias."

"Name?"

"Beltran." Shorty kept his eyes closed, his mouth a tight line.

"That a real name?"

He nodded.

"His office is in the bar."

"Where in the bar?"

"The bar. He uses the bar. He—" Shorty's voice shook.

"Thanks. I'll find him."

I wound up and gave him a knock like I did Zig the Tall-Boy. It wasn't perfect, but he tumbled off the chair, and it was like a goon sleep-over.

I didn't bother looking for the Colt they took off me. The Glock was a lot newer and conveniently held more bullets. I slid it into my holster, left the room, closing the door quietly behind me, and exited the hotel.

CHAPTER THIRTEEN

I WALKED OUT OF THE HOTEL without telling the front desk or checking out. The bill was with Morales and they could square it with him. I kept my stride swift, darting down a couple of side streets in close succession. I didn't think the goons from the room would follow, or not right away. But I didn't want to make it too easy for them.

I should have asked Shorty for the address to the Palomar, but I figured the hotels in Bucerias would be easy to find, since they all seemed to be gathered together. Scanning my surroundings and the buildings that rose up around me, I saw nothing that read *Palomar*. I stopped at a stand that had a large sign for Tecate beer. I thought I'd honor that invitation and pointed to it.

"Tecate. Pescado, dos."

At least I knew how to order fish tacos.

The woman behind the grill wore her curly hair piled high on her head, tied with a gold band. She reached into the cooler, pulled out an icy can, and handed it to me. She smiled broadly.

"Donde Hotel Palomar por favor?"

She smiled again but said nothing. I repeated myself.

"I'm sorry, señor, I do not speak Inglés."

Dammit. I thought I was speaking Spanish.

"Hotel Palomar." I said it slower, hiking up my shoulders in the universal sign that said I was an idiot.

Her expression brightened with awareness. I must have said it right by accident. She pointed to the street behind her and then made curving motions with her hand.

"Gire a la derecha después de dos cuadras."

She saw my little boy lost in the park expression and nodded. The woman reached for a napkin and took a pen out of her pocket. After a moment, she gave me the small map she'd sketched.

"Gracias."

"De nada."

The fish tacos had a few surprise peppers in them, so I had to order another Tecate to put out the fire. I considered whiling away the rest of the day like this, heat followed by wet and cold refreshment. Not a bad way to spend time.

Kitty corner to me, a street musician started strumming and singing in a soft tone. The cold cerveza and the hot peppers put me in a reflective mood. I touched the cut over my eye, already scabbed over, from where I took the guitar to the head. Couldn't speak Spanish worth shit, but at least I was a quick healer.

Sure. Okay. I knew I needed to help Benno's friend, associate, whatever. Benno would pay me tenfold whatever Morales gave me. And not just in money. Benno took care of me, more than any guy I had worked for—he was a true benefactor. He paid for both my hotel and bar bills, but I also had a feeling that he'd put the word out I was one of his. I couldn't point to any specifics, but I had seen how others had looked at me when I was in Benno's club.

Still, there were days that I knew being one of Benno's would not always help me. There was always going to be a guy with a gun and a bad disposition.

"Oh, you are one of Benno's? Well, suck on this."

Blam blam blam. End of Fischer. And damn, I liked that guy.

Carrying around the Colt, and now Shorty's Glock, put me in a mood. I hated carrying a gun. Thanks to a guy in the backwoods of Northern Ontario, I knew a lot about firearms and was a decent shot to boot. He'd trained me well. But it was like the gun radiated violence out of its metal shell and seeped into my veins.

I'd opened something up that wanted to stay closed. That much I knew. The meeting with Lopez in Sayulita was coincidental—though when you went looking for trouble, it usually found you first. I had gone to Sayulita planning to run into someone just like him, so I wasn't surprised when it led to me nearly getting my lights put out.

The visit from the mismatched goons was not an accident. Who calls somebody that big Zig? I laughed aloud at my unintentional mind rhyme, and the woman with the hair looked up. I ordered another Tecate, and she pulled another out of the icy cooler.

Someone knew that Morales, via me, was poking around. They wanted the poking to stop, and they wanted me to stop breathing. So why not just toss it in? Tell Morales I was sorry, but I came up empty. I could say the same to Benno. He'd understand, but he'd also know I was holding back. He'd know I was afraid of something, of failing, or worse. The guy had a sixth, and maybe a seventh, sense.

Mexico was a big country; Morales's daughter could be anywhere. This whole thing had the potential to be a lot more dangerous than any of the work Benno had me do. If people were owning and trading people, they were bound to be violent, aggressive, and willing to do whatever necessary to protect their interests.

So who were the sick fucks that did the trafficking? And who were the sicker fucks that bought? That wasn't much of a psychological summary, and it made me sound like a redneck vigilante who carries an axe wherever he goes—and not for chopping lumber. I'd heard someone call Mexico one of the largest sex tourism hubs in the world. Sure, I could enjoy an icy brew and chomp on tacos by the ocean. But all around me there was human sewage that made my guts burn.

The woman, who had been wiping the metal counter of her stand, looked up again. She put her hand on my shoulder and squeezed.

"Sorry, is there a problem? Problemo?"

"Tu cara está llena de preocupación. Es un día hermoso."

Another woman, much younger, barely out of her teens, watched our transaction.

"She says your face is full of worry. It is a beautiful day."

"Uh, thanks. I'm fine."

"No, no estás bien. Pero el dolor pasa como una tormenta."

"Sorry? Lo siento?" I asked.

"No, you are not fine. But pain passes like a rainstorm."

I considered that piece of wisdom and stopped myself from replying.

I lifted my can of Tecate to both women and nodded. No more needed to be said.

I finished my beer, turning to listen to the street guitar player. When I turned back, the two women were gone, so I had no one to say goodbye to.

Again, a darkness seeped into me. A shrink would say it was anxiety, and a shaman would tell me to pay attention. I once met someone who I believed was a shaman.

"Always listen. Always pay attention," he had told me.

More than the dark, it was a sense of something being torn away, removed from all else—the violence of the ocean swallowed humanity and spat it out like a lone surfboard washed up on the rocks. If I said that aloud to anyone, they'd think I was a prophet. Or an asshole. The difference was subtle.

The sun was sinking and the shadows were bleeding purple. I shuffled my way down the narrow Bucerias street. I studied the napkin map, made a couple more turns, and there it was, rising like an alabaster rollercoaster, topped off by white turrets that surely had medieval knights patrolling the boundary below. Climbing up the side were gold and bronze channel-letters spelling *PALOMAR*. The type on the sign should have read: money, and a lot of it.

The lobby was enormous. Lush plants rose from the marbled floors etched with black-and-white geometrics. A sweeping staircase wound around a burbling fountain, curving upward to places where only the rich could ascend. Standing there like a dirt farmer in a fairytale castle, I waited to be tossed out through the steel and glass doors.

When no one made a move to eject me, I made my way to the front desk, a long, curving teak job. The woman had high cheekbones and dark eye shadow that perfectly contrasted her crisp white shirt. At her collar she wore a thin black string tie. As I approached, she seemed wary, already guessing I didn't belong there.

"Pardon. I'm looking for a señor Beltran? I was told he is staying here."

"That is very familiar," she said. "Do you have the gentleman's forename?"

"His what?"

"What is the full name, señor?"

I took a few seconds too long before I said Hectore. It was worth a shot. The woman at the desk gave me what my mother would have called the Hairy Eyeball.

"I'm sorry, señor, we cannot give out the names of our guests staying at the Palomar."

"You just asked me for his name."

It was her time to hesitate. "I am sorry."

She turned her back to me and focused on a nonexistent task. *Shit.* Now I was going have to go back and beat another name out of Shorty and his statue-friend. I really didn't feel up to doing this. The open-aired room that stretched behind me had a bar at one end, and to the left a gorgeous view of the Pacific was framed by a pair of indoor palms that stretched up to where that staircase led. The place needed to have angel music pumped in to complete the effect.

I was about to ask the woman's back if anyone could drink in the Palomar lounge; some of the tonier places had rules about that. The hell with it—I needed some sustenance if I had to go back and talk to, then take on, the goons at the other hotel. I took a table on the edge with a great view of the crashing waves.

A group of horses appeared, led by a man in a black shirt and baseball cap. The lead animal was white with a tan mane. The letters *SF* were written on the hindquarters, maybe a brand or some kind of identifier. Muscles rippled under the animal's creamy coat. Nebraska Bob's face popped into my mind. I wondered if he ever did see a man about a horse. Another pair followed, with a small gray pony bopping along behind, the surf licking their hooves. I was so taken by the equine beauty that I didn't notice the server was right next to me.

"Señor?"

"Oh. Sorry. Dos cervezas por favor. Pacifico."

"Dos Equis, Modelo, y Corona."

I sighed.

"Modelo."

The horses padded their way down the beach; the little one raced ahead of the others. Their owners kept a close watch. They were not going to let any of them bolt. I admired the control and the relationship between them that I sensed, or maybe made up in my head.

"They are beautiful creatures, crafted by God himself," said a man in a tan, well-tailored suit one table over. His hair was perfectly coiffed, leading down to a pair of arrowed sideburns and a salt-and-pepper goatee sharp enough to cut bread.

"You saying God didn't do all the work around here? She had subcontractors?"

The man's laugh echoed in the wide space. He sipped at his tall brown drink, then dabbed his face with a cloth napkin. "You raise a good point. Perhaps I may join you to discuss this further?"

"It's a free country," I said.

"Is it?"

His tone was foreboding, like he had a secret to unload. A band across the back of my neck tightened, until he laughed again and extended his hand. I shook it.

"I am Santiago Beltran. Welcome to my office."

He waved his arm in a large circle.

"Nice place. How's the rent?"

"Ha. You have a very good sense of humor. For this reason I do not think you are American."

"I like to think of myself as local."

"Hmm. Not sure I would agree with that, señor Fischer."

"Do I know you?" Under the table, I clenched my fist.

"No. Not as of yet. I would ask you to put both your hands on the table."

I brought up my other hand, still clenched.

"I received a phone call only five minutes ago. I was informed you may be paying me a visit."

"Short guy, big lump on his head?"

A thin smile spread over his goatee—the kind I always had an urge to yank on to see if it was real.

"Let us begin by your telling me why you came to the Palomar. What are you looking for? Leave nothing out," Beltran said.

"Why would I leave things out?"

"I hold enough power in this area that if I were to shoot you dead in the middle of this hotel, all that would happen would be someone arriving to make your body disappear."

"Big man about town," I said.

"Enough of your jokes. Tell me your story."

I didn't doubt that Beltran was packing or the bit about shooting me in the hotel and no one giving a rip. I also didn't doubt he would do it before I was able to get Short's Glock out of the hip holster. As I didn't feel like being dead, or having my body carted off to some hidey-hole in the desert, I decided to spill it.

"I came looking for a young woman named Soleil, or maybe Sunny. Last name Morales."

Beltran tugged on his annoying beard. "I know of someone with this name, though her family name is different." He narrowed his gaze. "Is she a friend, a relative, a lover perhaps?"

"No. None of those."

"Come now, Fischer. I've asked you to not hold anything back."

"Or you'll lay me out on this nice tile. Looks like marble, must have cost a fortune."

Beltran slid his hand into his tan jacket in a gesture I supposed was a threat. "Continue."

"I was hired to find her by her father. First name Ramone, though he first told me it was Hectore."

"And why did he tell this lie?"

"Never figured that out," I said.

Something flashed in my table partner's face. It could have been recognition, but it was gone so fast, I wasn't sure. "I see."

He took his hand out of his jacket and a small pad with it. He scribbled on it, tore off the page, and slid it across the table.

"What's this?"

"Go to this address and seek out this man. He knows the Soleil you are looking for."

"Hmm. And what am I supposed to do with you?"

Beltran laughed. "I do enjoy your sense of humor. Are you from the United Kingdom? I can't place your accent."

"One of their properties," I said.

"I suggest, señor Fischer, that you go to this place. I'm assuming you have a firearm?"

"Good assumption."

"It is somewhat hidden under your loose clothes, but I am quite observant." Again, a flash of something across Beltran's face. His eyes were watery. "You are going into a center of violence with some very bad men. Some would call them evil, and they would not be wrong. In order to protect their interest, they would not hesitate to do what is needed."

"Like putting a bullet in my head."

"Among other places, yes."

I wasn't about to change this into a draw from the Old West. My Glock was shoved in the hip holster and rotated toward the back of my pants. I guessed Beltran had his near where he had pulled out the pad, a readily accessible shoulder holster, cross-draw for sure. Back of the pants versus jacket, the eternal question, and not just for tailors.

"I see that you are considering which path to take."

"I haven't heard a good argument against why Shorty would send me here," I said. "Then, when I find you in this luxury joint, you tell me I need to go find someone else."

"And therefore, you believe that this short man sent you to the one, what is that term … is behind it all?"

"He told me what I asked. I was quite convincing."

"I have no doubt," Beltran paused. "Señor Fischer, there is an adage I have learned. It is something that all great stories share in common."

"And what's that?"

"Nothing is as it seems."

I took this in. A breeze came up from the Pacific and blew through the large open room, drying the sweat on my neck. Santiago Beltran followed my gaze upward.

"Anything good to drink at this place?"

Beltran laughed. The guy did that a lot, not a damn care in the world when you have it by the tail. "You are at the birthplace of tequila, Fischer. And here at the Palomar they have a fine selection. They stock a reposado, aged eighteen years, that is very fine."

"Knew there was a reason I liked you, Beltran."

"Call me Santiago."

"Okay, Beltran." I held up the paper that he'd given to me. "Is this a street in Bucerias?"

"It is in Sayulita, a town north of here. By car it is perhaps thirty minutes."

"Longer by bus," I said.

"Ah. You have been there."

"Recently, yeah."

I spent the rest of the evening on Beltran's dime. The tequila flowed, and he was right, the aged reposado was damn fine. I also ordered a few rounds of cervezas, Modelos, though I still wished for Pacificos, as they helped with my thinking. Still, when someone else was paying I didn't need to get picky, as long as it wasn't that skunk-swill, Corona. When people thought of Mexican beer, they pictured those clear bottles with a lime jammed in the top, as if that could help the taste. Never could figure out why such a bad-tasting beer would be so popular.

Beltran said he had to leave to meet someone, but he would be back. He said to order whatever I liked, and he would take care of the bill. Like the bad beer, I couldn't figure this guy out. Shorty and his elongated pal obviously worked for him. But they weren't running the business I thought they did. I didn't know much about what traffickers looked like. Lucia's descriptions of the men could have fit the goons at the hotel, but not this Santiago guy. Though the guys at the top were always too clean and smelled too good.

It all felt off. The more I drank, the clearer my thinking got, like those damn Corona bottles. So what was the lime being shoved down my neck? Of course, like Beltran said, nothing was as it seemed. He hadn't filled in any gaps for me, either. So I was left with that hanging riddle.

After an hour, he returned to the lounge and sat across from me.

"I see you have been enjoying the hospitality," he said.

"You haven't told me how, or even if you know Morales, his daughter, or how they are tied into this place in Sayulita." I placed a finger on the paper that sat on the table between us. An image of a guitar being swung at my head flashed. "Wait. I might have been at this place."

"If you have been to this place, asking the questions that you have been asking, I do not believe we would be speaking right now."

"The bullet in the head thing, again?"

The server brought two small crystal glasses filled with a liquid the color of strong tea.

"I observe that you are someone who appreciates finer things. This is Clase Azul blended with a reposado finished in sherry casks from France."

I took a sip of the amber elixir and for a moment believed there was a God.

"I will end my evening here, señor Fischer."

"Oh, we are back to the niceties."

"And wish you a warm buenas noches. You are welcome to stay here at the Palomar. Then being refreshed, you can make your way to

Sayulita tomorrow morning. They make an excellent huevos rancheros here."

"Might need to call Morales and ask him. This is a bit more expensive than my usual digs."

"There is no need to call. It is taken care of."

"So this isn't just your office? You own the joint?"

Beltran smiled.

"You still haven't told me why you know my name. Or why you're giving me this address."

"I wish you a lovely night and a restful sleep. If I don't see you again, your family has my condolences."

"I'm sure they'd like that."

CHAPTER FOURTEEN

I WAS UP MUCH TOO EARLY. Thankfully, the coffee was dark and excellent. Beltran was right: they made a helluva good breakfast at the Palomar. The rich folks knew how to do it right, even though sitting in the open-air castle-like lobby made me feel the economic disparity in my gut. Well, a gringo's got to eat. And I felt like one this morning, stranger in a strange land and all that. I needed a task to focus on to get my blurry head on straight. I had one: find the girl, take care of the bad guys. I didn't know if I was up to either of them.

Beltran was nowhere to be seen, not that I expected him to be. The staff knew who I was and attended to me without ever asking for payment. One of the servers stopped me from leaving a tip.

"It has all been taken care of, señor. I am glad you enjoyed your stay at our hotel."

The kid was sneaking up on twenty, but the fuzz under his lip told me he was still in his teens. I wondered how someone his age got a job at a toney joint like this. Maybe he was related to Beltran. It's the kind of thing Benno would do for his family members.

I took another read of Beltran's piece of paper. He had never told me where in Sayulita the street was located. True, I should have asked him, but I hadn't expected to be heading back in that direction that fast. But I'd find it. Sayulita wasn't that big of town.

I must have caught one of the first segundas of the day; it was barely a third full. Could have been it was a Sunday, but I'd lost all track of the days of the week. I enjoyed the extra space and stretched out my arm to the empty seat.

I rode the bus all the way into the terminal this time. I tried to picture the spider web of Sayulita streets in my head, not wanting to rely on kids on bikes or muggers with knives for directions. I knew my way to the beach and figured I'd start there. I'd find one of the Sonnys that sold spots on the beach and ask them.

The morning waves were decent, and the faithful were out there cruising the Pacific froth. The for-sale chairs were mostly empty, and there were no Sonnys in sight. For sure when they appeared, they'd be chasing the stragglers who dared to sit in a chair for free. The bar was still closed. I paced down the beach, walking by a family, a mom and two little kids building sand castles.

"Excuse me," I started.

She held up a hand like she was trying to block the sun.

"No hablo inglés."

I was about to show her my piece of paper, but one of the kids destroyed the castle and now Mom was a referee in the middle of a full on fist battle.

"Gracias," I said over the yelling.

I kept going down the beach. Ahead were a few stalls lined up a small incline away from the beach. Hand-painted signs advertised surf-lessons: *ANY LEVEL. BEST IN SAYULITA*. The first stall was empty, as was the second, until a goddess of California walked out from a curtained-off space. That was my first thought when I saw her, blond hair tied in cornrows spilling off her shoulders, and she had long, tanned everything. She wore a pink bikini top over a pair of faded cut-offs the perfect shade of blue.

Her lips were full and her eyes would be at home in the best Botticelli painting. The shell she stepped out of must have been behind the curtain. When she smiled, her face opened like the sun dancing over the morning waves.

I needed a moment.

"Morning pal."

"Uh, hi."

She rotated her fingers like a beach magician and pointed a pair of index pistols at me.

"You look like a surfer," she said.

"Me? No. Just an admirer."

"Could have fooled me. You've got a surfer's body. Pretty sure you'd pick it up fast. Wanna go for a ride?"

"Uh. Maybe another time." I swallowed. "I was just looking for some directions."

"Beach is over there, ocean is just past. Wanna smoke a bowl?" Again, she hit me with the blazing smile.

I fumbled the paper out of my pocket, unfolded it, and held it out to her. She sat down in a lawn chair next to a small table with a clay pitcher and a red plastic cup. As she studied the paper, her brow furrowed, which had a strange effect on her smooth skin.

"Why do you want to go there?"

"Supposed to meet someone, but I don't know my way around Sayulita."

"You just get in? Not much happening this early."

"I see that."

"It will pick up, though. Always does. I get here early just to ease into the day."

"You're a surfing instructor."

"I teach a lot of things." She winked. "Hey, take a load off, tell me what news from the Shire."

"Come again?"

"Not a Tolkien fan, I take it. Well, never mind me. Listen, I've got a lesson in about," she leaned back and looked over her shoulder, "an hour or so."

As far as I saw, there was no time device back there.

"I got some lemon water, pour in a bit of tequila if that suits ya."

"Just looking for directions," I said.

"To that place on the paper? Why the hell would you want to go there?"

"You've been, then?"

"Not a great part of town. I'd take a wide berth around there during the day and totally miss it a night. Shit goes down that you don't want to know about. Whoever told you to meet you there isn't someone you should be meeting."

"What happened when you went?" I asked.

"I was with a guy for a while who knew some people over there. He took me to a party, if you could call it that. Mostly people drinking, doing lines, smoking crack, and that sort of shit. I'm no stranger to that scene, but when the knife fight broke out, it was time to scoot."

"Scoot?"

"Ha. Yeah." She picked up a blue pipe next to the pitcher. "Stick around, smoke a bowl with me, maybe I'll convince you to get on a board." She fired up the pipe and took a deep drag.

When a beautiful women asks you to stay … well, I gave it a thought.

"Just point me in the right direction," I said.

She blew out a cloud of thick smoke. "You really want to go there? Huh. You don't look like the type to stir up shit. Some sort of enforcer, maybe. I can smell cops, and you aren't one of those."

"Definitely not. I'm looking for someone."

"Bingo." She took another pull and snapped her fingers. She talked while she exhaled another cloud. "That's the vibe I was picking up. You're like one of those dudes that goes snooping around. A Pee-Eye." She extended the vowels. "You ever see that show where the guy has the cool car and wavy hair? You've got nice hair."

I laughed. "No. Never saw that one. And I'm not a detective of any sort. I was asked to go to that address."

"Asked by who?"

"Someone who lost something," I said.

She gave a long slow head gesture, somewhere between a nod and a bass groove.

"Okay, man of mystery. Go back on this street, up this way." She pointed to the pathway that led away from the row of stalls. "Hang a left and walk until you run out of street. There's a ratty clothing shop there named Mickey's. Walk south from there a block and then one more left. That's the street. You want me to draw it out?"

"No, I'm good."

She held out the pipe for me, and I took it this time. I inhaled a citrusy smell mixed with a woodsy taste.

"Yeah, I bet you are." She gave me a long wink, laughed, and took the pipe back.

The weed was strong, giving me an immediate head rush. I gave her a quick nod of thanks and headed up the path. Her instructions banged around my brain. They were simple enough, should be no problem.

I could have explained why I wanted to go to the place she told me to avoid. Me holding back was a barometer of the lack of trust that bubbled in my guts. I couldn't put my finger on it, but something was off. Like Beltran said, nothing was ever what it seemed. Oldest damn story in the book, and it still took me too long to realize it.

CHAPTER FIFTEEN

I WALKED TO THE END of the street and found the clothing shop the surfer girl had mentioned. It was called Malley's, so she was close on the name. As I turned to go south, a familiar face came out of the shop.

"Fischer, what the hell are you doing here?"

It was Indiana Bob, or wherever he was from. He looked a lot rougher than the last time I'd seen him—or really any time I'd ever seen him. His shirt was a wrinkled mess, his hat looked like someone had stepped on it, and he had circles under his eyes that were too dark to be from tiredness. It looked like he went three rounds with a middleweight champ.

"Thought you were in Bucerias, Bob?"

"Sure was. And that's why I came here after." Bob took a long blink, trying to focus or stay upright. One of his knees started to buckle before he righted himself.

"You okay, Bob?"

"Hey, Fish-man, you up here looking for horses, too? They got some fine ones in Si-yoo-lita."

He stretched out the vowels as he talked. Bob slid his hand under his hat, knocking off the short fedora, and ran his fingers through his greasy hair. He coughed, and I reached down to pick his hat off the street.

"Horses are your deal, Bob."

I handed him his hat, and he jammed it on his head.

"Ha. So, what, you're here for surfing lessons? Yer such a fucking tourist." He stumbled on a cobblestone, and I caught him before he kissed the rocks.

"Easy."

"I'm fine, Fish-cat." He pushed me off and regained his balance. "Where you headed?"

"Mariposa Street."

"No shit. I just came from there. So you're a horse lover after all."

"Sure."

"Hey, Fish-turd. You ever been to Nebraska?"

Right, that was where he was from. Nebraska Bob pivoted and then strode ahead of me so fast, I had to move quick to keep up. Everything felt off about him. Could have been drugs, or someone had smacked him around hard. Whatever he'd taken didn't slow his pace at all—he was driving like a hopped-up bulldozer. If anything or anyone got in his way, he'd plow them over.

Despite what he said, I didn't think we were going to the same place—but I also knew we weren't talking about regular horses. Something burbled inside me that told me things were about to get bats in a cave dark.

"How long were you in Bucerias, Bob?"

Bob was in his own world and ignored my question. He put his hand up in the air and waved his finger, making a circle like he was leading a parade.

"You know people here in Sayulita?" I asked.

"I know everyone."

"What are the horses, Bob?"

He laughed. "You know what they are, Fish-jack."

As we walked, the number of buildings with boarded-up or broken windows increased. The sidewalk disappeared, replaced by a worn, wooden boardwalk. Then that was gone, too.

I tried to make conversation with Bob, but he remained cryptic. At one point he spouted a long diatribe on personal freedom. He'd be damned if the government was going to impose their fascist agenda on him. Line the bastards up against the wall and he'd execute every last one of them.

I interrupted and asked him which government he was talking about.

"All of them."

He barked a huge laugh, followed by a string of coughs.

"You okay, Bob? Maybe we should stop for a bit. Rest. I'm in no hurry."

"What do you think of morality, Fischer? Where do you get it from? Is it inside or outside?"

"Helluva question." It stopped me that he called me by my actual name.

"Exactly."

Before I could answer him, a skinny man in ragged clothes approached us. He spoke in fast, yet quiet, Spanish. Bob pushed the man back, hard.

"Fuck off!"

Bob took a wild swing and clipped the man on the shoulder and chin. He whimpered and fell to one knee.

"No más. No más."

Bob drew back, and I saw that he was about to kick the man while he was down.

"Bob! What the hell?"

I grabbed his shoulders and yanked him back. The skinny guy, stood, then tottered off as fast as his undernourished body would allow.

"Where the fuck are you going?" Bob pulled away from me and spun around. "Hey, are you following me? Who the fuck are you?"

"Bob, settle down, it's me. Fischer. What did you take?"

"Huh?"

He shook his head like a cartoon character trying to focus.

"Sons of bitches gave me something," he said. "Tequila, mezcal, or something else. It was spiked. Had to be."

"Who did?"

"Fischer?" A light flashed in Bob's eyes. "Luke? What are you doing here?"

If I had a glass of water, I'd have thrown it in his face—not that it would have done any good.

"What are these horses you're looking for?"

"Horses? Oh yeah, they are fine, lovely things. Young and so fine."

"Oh, shit." I was starting to put it together.

"C'mon, Fish-Cat. Let old Bobbie show you the way." He tugged on my sleeve, but then, after a few steps, he stopped. "But listen, if they offer you a drink … pass on that."

"Sounds like a plan."

A cross-street appeared out of a cloud of dirt and dust. A three-wheeled vehicle emerged from it, taking a wide turn and peeling ahead of us. When the dust cleared, I made out a mottled white-and-brown adobe house. Metal grills covered the windows. A porch hung off the building, looking like it would slide into the street at any moment. A guy with a huge square head wrapped in a green bandana yelled across to us.

"Is that you, Bob? Amigo. We wondered where you got to."

Two others joined him on the narrow porch. One held a broad knife with a fat handle, the other wore a muscle shirt. Dark ink tattoos circled his thick forearms.

"Friends of yours?" I asked.

"Listen, you sons-of-whores. I paid you in full. There was no need." Bob spat out his words.

"No need for what, amigo?"

"You know goddamn what."

"Ha! You are like the other one who came back. They always come back."

"No more fucking around."

Bob's voice had straightened. Whatever was in him had either disappeared or cranked up his body another notch. I wanted to ask who the other one was. Something creeped inside me that told me who it was.

Bob rushed the one in the bandana. I didn't expect the burst of strength from him. He tackled the guy to the ground and started punching him in the face. A piss shiver went through me as I considered how long before I'd have to make a move.

For what seemed like too many seconds, the others on the porch stared at the spectacle. The one with the tattooed arms laughed. The one with the knife jumped on Bob's back and the guy underneath bucked. Bob yelled as he was flipped over. In a blur of activity, Bob was up on his knees, his eyes as wide as dinner plates and the blade up against his throat.

"Hold on a second—"

Bob didn't finish his sentence before the guy whipped the knife down and stuck it in his side. Bob said *whoof* or something like it.

I took a step, reaching behind my back to slide the Glock from the holster. Tattoo-guy stopped laughing, raised a pistol, and pointed it between my eyes.

"Stop moving, señor."

I hadn't even noticed the guy was carrying. The whole situation was going into the shitter. The one who Bob had recently pummeled was off the ground now. His lip was split and his eyes red and puffy. He hacked up something and spat it on Bob.

Nebraska Bob lay on his side, breathing hard. The one with the blade toed him with a weathered boot.

"You should have kept walking, Mr. Bob," he said. "You did not play nice like the señor. He paid the full price, and he has what is his again."

"Look. I'm not wanting to start anything. But he's going to need some medical attention." I pointed at Bob, whose skin was turning a bad color.

"Attention?" Blade-guy laughed and gave a salute. "We will let him die in the street." He straightened his bandana. "If you are his friend, maybe you should pay his bill."

"Not that good of a friend," I said. "Don't even really know the guy."

Bandana-guy clucked his tongue. "No loyalty for a friend? Señor, that is no way to live."

I studied the three of them. There was no weight shifting to suggest they were about to come at me. We were like a bunch of men just shooting the shit in the street while the guy on the ground bled to death.

"Did he owe a gambling debt?"

Bandana-guy exchanged a fast glance with his partners. "No. Not gambling. Mr. Bob made a purchase from us, but he did not pay in full. We need to be paid."

"Like the other señor. The one inside," I said.

"You know the other one? Friends with him, too?"

"No."

"Ha. You seem like you could be friends. He likes the young ones."

"For Bob there was the nose powder," the one with the pistol added.

"Yes, he did. Of course, from our previous times together. So the bill is quite high now."

Bob moaned and then let out a string of curses.

"We can get this settled. But listen, he's dying. Have a heart."

I don't know why I bothered to say such a strange thing. It's like I was asking them to help an injured dog, and my voice skipped when I said it.

The one with the pistol swung away from me and fired three times into Bob. The air was way too still. The gun's report echoed in my ears.

"That is what I think of his heart," he said. "Listen. It is no longer beating."

I split a second into two halves. The first part was sadness for Bob, the second half I pivoted hard on my back foot and bolted down the street. I waited to feel a bullet between my shoulder blades, but none came. Going against the thoughts I carried and the burning in my guts, I ran away from the place I should have stayed. I knew who was in the house.

CHAPTER SIXTEEN

I TOOK THE FIRST RIGHT I SAW and headed down another side street, more of a narrow alley. As a kid, I'd have called this a pass-through. Out into the open area I leaped over a sleeping dog, then skidded to a stop on the gravel and dirt street. A quick look back showed the dog was still asleep, but more importantly, none of the porch goons had followed me. Or not yet.

From what I could tell, and based on some quick goon math, I didn't have much of a chance of finding my way into that house. I noted, before they ended poor Bob's life, that the address was the same one Beltran had given me. I cranked my head toward a dog's bark. One of the goons appeared in the alley. It was the one who stabbed Bob. He didn't attempt to leap over the dog like I did. Instead, he gave it a boot with his dirty sneaker.

Sure, the dog looked his age, but it was still a bad choice. The hound jumped up barking and then was on the guy. The goon had his knife out, but the dog chomped down on his wrist and ended that advantage. If I was a betting man, my money was solely on the one with four legs and a mouthful of teeth.

Watching the dog versus goon battle, and definitely rooting for the dog, I took stock of my situation. I was in a dusty little alley running away from a violent shit show. A friend, okay, acquaintance of mine was lying dead in the street. Chances are we would have shared a hole if I hadn't bolted.

The whole time I watched Bob go after it, and then get taken down, the Glock had stayed in the back holster under my shirt. Why? It was a damn good question. I could have taken one or two of them down fairly quickly—not sure if more goons would appear out of that clown car of a house. Something like guilt still burbled and burned in my gut. *Dammit.* Bob was never going back to Nebraska.

True, I was ready to pitch the whole enterprise. None of this was worth a ticket to the heavenly choir. Beltran, and even Benno, be damned. Where the hell was Benno anyway? What a time to decide to go to Cuba, or Canada, or Timbuktu. I needed him to release me from this whole deal.

I felt as out of place as a figure skater at a monster truck rally. I was doing a whole different double-axel.

The goon had finally kicked the dog off him. Lines of blood ran down his arms and across his face. The dog arched, ready for another, probably final, lunge. The goon brought a gun out of his coat and aimed at the dog's head. The dog recognized something, a firearm, and tilted his head to the side. He let out a low woof.

I whipped out my Glock and fired two shots, one in the goon's head, the other in his neck. The dog pissed himself. I don't blame him. I would have done the same.

"Dammit."

So much for pitching the whole situation. In for a penny, in for a ton.

I ran back in the direction I came, taking a wide berth around the dead goon. The dog looked at me with tired but wise eyes.

"Good boy."

There was still no one in the alley, but with the sound of the shots, I guessed I wouldn't be alone for long. My walk through the pass-through turned into a jog. It wasn't like I had a single plan in my head, but an engine had fired up within me. I knew what it was—the one that always chugged deep below the surface. Since my days of beating heads in parking lot fights or hammering sparring partners in Montreal, I'd been able to suppress the thrum, even push it deeper. It was the sleeping giant, not snoring, sawing metaphorical logs, but dormant. Inactive. Seeing the goon about to kill the dog, it awoke. The giant had a name. Rage.

I quickened my pace coming out of the pass-through, scanning left and right. A few people were scattered on the street. Three smoked cigarettes and talked to each other in spurts of fast Spanish. A woman carried a basket of oranges, maybe freshly picked, their dark green leaves a stark contrast with the pile of almost-red fruit. I peeled past her, not even bothering to put away the gun I still held. The engine pushed away all my mental faculties, forcing them into one arrow of purpose. Go back to the house. Stop whatever was happening there. No matter what, stop it from happening. Now.

Someone yelled in Spanish, probably directed toward me. I heard the words *gringo* and *loco*. I didn't hear any footfalls behind me, and I didn't bother to turn and look.

One more turn and I was back at the adobe house. The grilled windows were like black teeth against the peeling wall. The door on the porch closed with a bang. Bob's body was gone—a dark trail went in the direction of the house. Even as I sprinted, I made out these details in crystal clarity, my senses sharp, my brain dull, except for the drive of the engine. No time for thought, only purpose. It was time to lay it all out.

A goon came out the door he'd just gone in. His hand dipped in his jacket and brought out a snub-nose. I shot him in the chest. I pushed past his collapsed body, around a rusted bench, through the door, and into the house. The giant was on fire and let out a bellow that I barely recognized as my own voice. Two men jumped up from their chairs. I shot one in the hip. He spun and went to the floor. The other raised his hands.

"No mas. Alto."

I dropped my bead on him. The goon lowered his hands, a bit too quick, which told some hidden part in my brain all I needed to know. He jerked out his pistol, but I was a second faster and shot him in the forehead. He flew back as if pulled by a rope.

"Sure. No mas. Right."

All around me, and even more inside, a heat sizzled, the fire threatening to explode out of my chest and burn everything in its wake.

"All right, you peckerwoods. Come out, and you better throw out your guns or I'll cut you down like the fuckers you are."

The crickets and mice went silent. A board creaked, and I spun around. I was alone in the room. Another creak came, and I traced it to the porch outside. Through the dirty grated window I made out the rusted bench. It was a glider on a track. The wind must have moved it. I didn't recall even a breeze as I'd run down the street to the house. But would I feel it in my current state? A vague confusion drifted through my mind for a full three seconds before a shadow on the porch shook. With an explosion of glass, the room erupted in gunfire. I dove to the floor. Shots rang out, busting all manner of things over my head.

The window shooter bust through the door, and a funny thing happened, but there was no time to laugh. The goon made a bad step and slipped on the lone rug in the room. He face-planted hard onto the wooden floor. He looked up with a dazed look, and I shot him.

"Fuck."

Even in the middle of the blaze burning in my body, a river of sadness curled and bled through me. This was not who I was. Good God.

But they had awakened the giant. Shards of glass covered the floor where I was still stretched out. I rose carefully, nicking my thumb. A line of blood bloomed and dripped on the floor.

Someone groaned, then muttered in Spanish. It was the first guy I'd taken down at the hip. Behind him was a narrow door that I'd missed when first entering. It was the same color as the wall on either side. Voices lifted up, a woman's pitch, and then another lower tone. Like someone flipped a switch and the sound disappeared. I stared at the door.

CHAPTER SEVENTEEN

I MOVED AROUND THE HIP-SHOT GUY to the door at the back of the room. I almost wanted to apologize. Almost.

"Puta," he mumbled.

"Yeah, I know."

The door where I'd heard voices was locked. I pushed on it with my body. The wood felt thin, but it wasn't budging. I'd kicked at doors before and ended up with a sprained ankle, so I wasn't doing that again. I aimed at the latch and fired. A kick in the hole left by the bullet and I was through.

The room was square, holding a water-stained table with tipped-over glasses, a bottle on its side, the red contents forming a puddle that dripped onto the floor. A shuffle of feet behind me, and another mutter of puta.

I turned and fired. Hip-shot guy was now neck-shot guy. He toppled to the floor, and his gun spilled out of this hand. I grabbed it. He was now dead-guy, and I cringed to hear myself think this. *Yeah, you're a fucking riot, Fischer.* The giant was not asleep, but quiet, somber. Both of us had had enough of death.

A hum in the room lifted up. I wasn't sure if something electric was buzzing or it was my imagination. Music came from somewhere, guitar strings, a shaker rhythm, a sad Spanish singer. The single window, this one ungrated, poured light in from the outside. The door at the back of this room was ajar. I pushed it open and then immediately stepped back. All I needed was a goon to jump up like a jack-in-the-box and end my breathing. And shit, I liked breathing.

I edged outside. The first thing I saw was Bob's crumpled body shoved against a low brick wall. Son of a bitch. My stomach lurched, and I threw up my long-ago breakfast huevos. I wiped my mouth, and as my eyes adjusted to the brightness, I saw the two of them ahead. He was trying to run, but the woman he pulled along slowed him down. I knew I'd find him. I had no doubt he would be here—her, I wasn't so sure. The realization had slipped in somewhere after the surfer girl and before the death of Nebraska Bob. I'd been suckered. Daughter, my Canadian ass.

"Morales."

My voice sounded too loud for the street, echoing off the cobblestones, rising into the sky it bounced off a low-flying pelican. It stopped him. I was too far away to see the glaze in his eyes, but I knew it was there—the look of a wild animal driven by forces he no longer tried to contain. He yanked on the woman again and barked at her. She had no choice but to join him in his run. I took off after them.

Whatever music I'd heard, real or in my head, was gone. Feet on the dirt pounded, my breaths in and out, focused like bellows, feeding the fire. Morales ducked down the first side-street. He moved faster than I thought he was capable—could be he'd lied about that, too. The bastard pretended to be old. I no longer know anything. It didn't matter.

I told my aching legs to quiet and churned after Morales and the one he pulled along. The pair ran through a street stall, knocking a box of mangoes to the ground. The vendor scrambled and yelled as the fruit bounced. I had to swerve around him, and I almost bit it when I slipped on a squished mango. Morales burst past a pair of older women laden with bags. More yells and someone screamed. It could have been the woman he ran with. The girl. She was too young to be called anything else.

My chest was tight, too long since I'd pushed my heart and lungs like this. I took in a long breath, centering myself, listening again to the rhythm that calmed me. As I sprinted, barely aware of the sound of my feet pounding the stones, internal music came back. It was a soft yet driving melody. The singing was words I still didn't understand, but I didn't need to. I raised my gun and shouted.

"Morales."

If I risked a shot, I could hit her. No way I could trust myself at this speed. They ducked under an awning. I was almost upon them, yards, feet, steps too few to count. Then I was in the air, pain shot through my ankle. I'd tripped over something—a wayward piece of concrete. When I hit the ground, she spun away from him. My body hit the ground but the adrenalin wouldn't let me feel the pain. Not just yet. I swore under my breath, muttered something to the god of targets, fired, and hit him right below the knee. It wasn't pretty, but I didn't give a single fuck. Morales tumbled and crashed into a table laden with bananas. It was almost funny. But it wasn't. The owner of the stall started to say something fast in Spanish, then changed his mind and ran off. Under the awning it was the girl, me, and the bastard who started all of this. We were alone on a dusty street.

Time went weird. What now?

"Señor?"

Her voice quavered. She was also on the ground, her eyes wide. She stood, and I knew she was about to bolt.

"Wait. Está bien … just wait."

I held up my hand. Her eyes darted. Morales tried to stand and failed.

"You're a son of a bitch," he seethed.

"Yeah. Well, one of us is."

Pain rippled over his face. "I no longer need your help." He said it like I didn't know every single fucking thing he said was a lie. "I've telephoned señor Benno to say that I found her."

"You don't know Benno. And you never have."

"But, mi hija."

"Don't call her that, you piece of shit."

The girl, Soleil, was speaking softly in Spanish. For a hummingbird second I looked at her.

"Está—"

That's all it took. Morales reached into his jacket so quick, I barely saw the flash of metal. I moved, but not fast enough. The flying blade slashed me just above the elbow. The burning pain spun me around, and I fell to one knee. I didn't drop the gun. I tightened my grip and aimed at Morales.

"Shoot. Kill him. I hate him. Kill."

Soleil spat the words out like curses.

"So that's the English you know?" I asked her. "I've had enough of this."

I got to my feet. Morales grasped his wound.

"My daughter doesn't understand. You need to leave us be—now. I will take care of her."

"I told you, don't call—"

"Fire at him. El cerdo. El cerdo."

"Yeah, I heard you the first time. Listen, here's what's going to happen. Me and you are leaving." I pointed at Soleil. "And *you* can just stay on the ground and bleed until someone comes and finds you. It won't be anyone from the house, unless there's someone I didn't shoot. Maybe it will be the policía. I don't care."

I tucked the gun into the back holster and moved next to Soleil. She wore a loose blouse made of a light fabric.

"Excuse me for a second," I said.

"You are a pig. El cerdo."

"Just hang on."

I ripped a strip of fabric from her shirt, exposing a soft, tanned belly.

"Help me with this," I said to her.

She understood. I took the strip and wrapped it around my slashed arm. The white of the fabric bloomed with blood.

"Let's go."

"You'll not shoot him?"

"I'm tired of shooting."

"I will do it."

I sighed. The exhaustion I felt in every ounce of my body almost overran the hot pain of the cut. Almost. I'd be lying to myself if I didn't think about handing her the gun. Morales had made me a sucker. He deserved to die in the street.

"Let's go."

I took her by the arm and went down the narrow Sayulita road. The dust lifted as we walked. If Morales said something to us as he moved away, I didn't hear it. There might have been a scramble of people behind us. But I didn't hear that either. Somewhere really far away, like miles, a guitar player strummed a soft rhythm and sang a peaceful melody. It was all in Spanish, of course. It didn't matter. I followed the sound. Soleil was quiet. Maybe she heard it too.

CHAPTER EIGHTEEN

WHERE'S A COP WHEN YOU NEED ONE? I couldn't remember where I'd heard or read that. Some old TV show. Being in Mexico, the question was about the policía. While I walked fast with Soleil's arm in mine, the phrase popped into my head.

Right now, the last thing I needed was some form of law enforcement to show up and point guns at my head before any questions were asked. I knew corruption flowed through many of the forces, but like anywhere, there'd be a group of honest cops. Or that was the hope. If I told them that I'd just rescued this woman from a life of sexual slavery, they'd listen, understand, and bring in some professionals to provide counseling, then take Soleil to a safe place where she'd recover from her trauma. Or if they were being paid by the traffickers, they'd shoot me in the head and be done with it.

I found my way back to the only place I knew might offer some refuge. When I came into her stall, she was there with another woman. I worried it was a customer, and I'd have to wait. I didn't have time to wait. When the other woman turned, I saw the family resemblance. Without a word exchanged they came to me, softly speaking in Spanish and then in English.

"You can come to our home. Estarás bien." Lucia's tone was warm.

"¿Dónde está Celestina?"

The woman who must be Lucia's mother spoke with a trembling voice. At the sound of the name, Soleil's eyes widened.

"Si. Yo la conocia."

Words were exchanged, and though I watched the body language and expressions, I didn't really know what they were talking about.

"She said that she met my sister at one of the places she was kept. That was two months ago, and she hasn't seen her since that time. She said she was very beautiful and strong."

"Yes, she was," Soleil said.

"¿Hablas inglés?"

Soleil nodded, and Lucia's mother brought her into an embrace.

"Venga conmigo."

As they left the tented stall, Soleil turned to me. "Thank you." Her eyes were soft.

Somewhere out in the street, a siren rose up. I hadn't heard one for a long time. I knew the sound, but at the same time I didn't. Again, waves of exhaustion swam through me. They lifted up like the siren, threatening to drown me. I swallowed hard, not wanting to lose myself in front of Lucia. My legs struggled to keep me upright.

"You are injured," she said.

A cold sweat broke across my forehead. I fought back the urge to throw up.

Lucia guided me to a chair. She took a cloth, dipped it in a bowl of water, and drew it across my face and neck. She unwrapped the bloody fabric of Soleil's blouse. From underneath a table she brought out a small basket.

"I cannot stitch it, but this will help."

Lucia cleaned the wound and taped it with steri-strips. She dressed it with a thin layer of gauze and a wide bandage. She gave me a small tube from the basket.

"Keep this clean, apply this ointment to prevent infection. Will you stay in Sayulita?"

"Not a good idea," I said.

"I have a cousin who will drive you where you need to go."

"I can just take a bus."

"That is not a wise decision. Those who you confronted will be there."

"How do you know I confronted anyone?"

"It is written on your face. And your arm." She smiled and reached for my hand. "You are Luke."

"You have a good memory."

"Go down this street." She pointed out the stall. "The last house on the corner has a palapa awning. There is a blue door. Go inside, stay there, and my cousin will come."

Someone strummed a guitar and sang softly. It was coming from the stall next to the one where I stood with Lucia. I wondered if he was the one I'd heard.

"Okay," I said.

"He will give you fresh clothes. You cannot travel like this." Lucia pointed at a spray of blood, not mine, that I hadn't noticed. "Drink this. The sweetness will be good for you."

She handed me a bottle of the horchata I'd had before. I took a long swallow.

"Maybe he could drive me to Bucerias. I can take a bus from there."

"He will take you wherever you need to go," she said.

"I don't really know where."

"Then you can think on the way."

Another siren sounded, drowning out the guitar player. I nodded and stood, feeling the steadiness return to my legs. Lucia took both my hands, brought them to her face, and kissed them.

"I'm sorry about your sister."

"We will continue to hope. Go now."

I went down the street to the house with the thatched awning. On the narrow porch, an old man sat on an overturned bucket. He peeled an apple, letting the skin fall on the wooden slats.

"Lucia sent me."

He touched his weathered hat and pointed to the open blue door behind him. I waited in a small room. Light poured in through a pair of windows illuminating a row of green plants. The closest one had flowers the color of the sun.

There was the rumble of an engine on the street. A man entered, slightly older than Lucia, with a thick mane of hair. He handed me two shirts and a pair of dark pants. He pointed to the door and left. He got lucky with the pants size. I took the shirt that best matched my mood. Lucia's cousin revved the engine, and I changed quickly.

CHAPTER NINETEEN

LUCIA'S COUSIN, Mateo, spoke little English. He seemed serious, gruff even, but as we left Sayulita he pulled up next to a pair of kids on bikes. They weren't the ones I'd come across before, but they both had those wild faces of youth. They shouted at my driver, who laughed and shouted back. He reached into a cup and threw some pesos out the window. Then he blew them a raspberry and laughed again. The kids jumped off their bikes and grabbed at the coins scattered on the road. Mateo spoke fast to me, maybe saying something about the kids. I said *Bueno*, because it's all I could think of to say.

My arm where I was cut throbbed. But I was a quick healer, and I knew Lucia's dressing was done well. I fingered the tube of antibiotic I'd put in my breast pocket. I'd given the Glock and holster to the old man on the porch. He'd nodded his thanks.

As we drove the winding roads, my eyes grew heavy. I was too tired to worry about being followed by the policía or more goons or really anyone. I was drifting, falling asleep, when Mateo spoke a few of the English words he knew.

"Where to, señor?"

It was the third time he'd asked me since we left Sayulita.

When I didn't respond, he asked, "Vallarta?"

"Melaque."

It popped into my head. I must have been half-dreaming. I didn't expect him to drive me somewhere that would take three hours or more to get there.

"San Patricio?"

I recalled the local name for it.

"Yes. San Patricio."

"Si."

"Okay?"

The kindness of people had a way of surprising me. It shouldn't anymore, since I'd met so many people in this country that exuded an openness I'd found in few places.

"Si. It is beautiful," Mateo said.

"Yes. It is."

"Pelícano."

"Sure."

He turned on the car radio, and gentle drums began a shuffling rhythm. The sun had started its descent, and already the sky had shifted into purple hues. Above the tree line I made out the shape of a lone heron, its beak pointed like an arrow to my destination. Mateo tapped on his steering wheel and hummed along.

When I awoke, a fat moon hung in the sky like the softest yellow custard shining down on a line of lush *parota* trees. A row of low buildings appeared, leading to a bus station that I recognized. Behind the station, I made out the lit clock tower that rose above the square. I imagined its chimes a moment before they began to ring.

"Melaque," Mateo whispered.

The music had been shut off, though I still heard the rhythm in my head.

"There's a place up there. Across from the terminal." I pointed out the window. "The Monterrey."

"Si."

He pulled up next to the hotel with the large yellow arch and stopped. I searched my jacket for some money. He held up his hand to stop me and then reached across to shake my hand.

"Vaya con dios."

***

I GOT A ROOM ON THE SECOND FLOOR, smiling at the familiar surroundings, the striped bed coverings, the braided rug, and the open windows. The Pacific thrummed, and that custard moon had grown white as it climbed high above the water.

The next days moved at a pace that I had longed to return to. I slept late, drank the cinnamon-laced coffee, and ate slices of ripe papaya before wandering onto the beach to watch the pelicans fish. Throughout the day, they dove from great heights, snatching their catch from the ocean. I have no idea how they could spot the fish below all that water. But they were ancient creatures and had done this for eons. One morning, I stripped down and waded in to join the birds. I didn't plan on fishing, I just needed to be submerged in water and close to them. I'd taken Lucia's dressing and the strips off last night. The cut had already formed into a long, bumpy scab. I kept my boxers on, not wanting to offend people or scare the hell out of the decent family who had laid out a row of chairs to enjoy the ocean view. The youngest kid pointed to a pelican as it dived only a couple of yards from me. He laughed as I was sprayed with the water from the plunge.

After a long, languid morning, I went to the market for tacos and more fruit. I knew where to find the best coffee, next to a small bookstore that carried a few American novels. I was surprised to find a Travis McGee paperback on one of the wire racks. I went with my coffee and book to the square, found a bench under a wide tree, and transported my mind to the Florida Keys. I made a mental note to go there some day.

I tried to disappear into the book as the morning heat lifted around me. Servers at a taqueria had begun to set out white plastic chairs, and children raced across the square. One server playfully swatted at a kid who knocked over one of the chairs. When the kid squealed, I jumped and dropped my book.

I'd tried to find my rhythm again, the pace that allowed me to slide into a day like I'd slipped into the ocean with the pelicans. The streets of Melaque had a calming effect on me, as did the people I saw, talked with, shared a Pacifico with at a palapa. But the unease, or, more accurately, the *disease* was still there. I didn't know what it would take to remove it.

I left the square and wandered down to a quiet café a few blocks north. There were only two tables in the place. At one, a man sat hunched over an espresso cup and smoked a hand-rolled cigarette. A thick black dog sat at his feet. The man ruffled the dog's fur with his free hand. When I went to sit at the other table, he beckoned to me, gesturing to the chair across from him.

I joined him, and before I could order, the server had placed down a cup the same size and style as his. A deep, earthy smell came from the espresso.

"I guess you were waiting for me," I said.

"We have never met, señor," he said in a thick accent.

"I was joking."

The dog came over and rubbed against my leg.

"This is Noa. She is kind."

"Like all of Melaque's dogs," I said.

I sipped the dark brew, thankful that a light breeze had lifted up. Someone was frying tortillas somewhere. A rooster crowed. The whole town was run by roosters and dogs. Though they never seemed to bother each other.

"You are troubled," he said.

"We all are."

He didn't smile. "Not like you are. I can see this."

The lines around his eyes radiated across his smooth skin.

"You're Melaque's prophet then?"

"I am Antonio. I have seen you in the square. You walk as if you are dragging a weight."

I wanted to make a wiseass crack about the heat, but there was something in his gaze that stopped me.

"Do you live here?" I asked.

"I have a place on the sand. Perhaps you've seen it when you swim with the pelicans."

"You've been following me?"

An image flashed in my head of a lean-to structure I'd passed a couple of days ago. It sat high up on the beach, far enough that the tide wouldn't reach. It was put together with metal, wooden posts, and sheets of burlap.

"Tell me of the weight," Antonio said.

"Why?"

Antonio made a clicking sound, and Noa went to him. He stroked her head, and without looking at me, he said, "There are people who live at a high frequency and those who live in a low frequency. You must decide which one you will choose."

And that was it. He got up and walked away. The dog followed, and neither looked back. I finished my small cup and went to pay. The server waved me off, saying only, "Antonio."

I wandered down another dirt road. Two more dogs passed me. I both knew and didn't know what Antonio meant. Betrayal was a bitch; maybe that's what he saw on my face. Why did I believe Morales in the first place? I'd thought I was smarter than that.

I wound my way through the streets. Melaque's sun-dried adobes reflected the shifting moods that coursed through my body. Never been much of a philosopher, but the town made me ponder something beyond words. I passed an aqua-blue building saddled up next to the yellow ochre house where the sun bounced and intensified the hues, and then a bright pink building where I knew I could get hot bolillos in the morning. A trio of kids on bikes spun by a tall apartment painted half-mauve, half olive-green and bordered by a bright white balcony. All these colors soothed the parts of me broken by the past.

Without planning, I found myself under the clock tower, now casting a shadow across the arc of brick benches that circled the square. As if in answer to my walking daydream, a row of brightly colored triangle flags fluttered in the wind, strung across the main square in preparation for whatever would be taking place that night. There was always something to celebrate. I sat on the benches directly below the arrows of color. When I saw him coming across the square, I noticed the fedora first. A lemon-yellow number that reminded me of last night's moon. I shouldn't have been surprised, so I wasn't.

"You're back from wherever you were."

"It is good to see you, my friend."

"Where?"

"I had an extended stay at some islands. A time of rest."

"A communist island?"

Benno smiled and joined me on the bench. "I have a cousin who works here at the hotel. He called me to say you were staying here."

"He just called you out of the blue? Or are you keeping tabs on me?"

Benno put his hand on my knee and patted it. "How are you, my friend? I have heard of some troubles. North of here."

Trust Benno to always know what was happening.

"He told me he was an associate of yours," I said.

A look of confusion spread across my benefactor's face, and then he nodded with realization.

"Ah, of course. You are speaking of R. Morales. I am sorry that happened, Luke. I know of this man but have never conducted any business with him. I believe he came to know someone under my employment. From that relationship, he discovered some information."

"Information? About me?"

"It would seem. Yes."

It was my turn to smile.

"So I have a bit of a reputation with your crew?"

"You've helped us in many ways. And you have helped me, my friend." Benno leaned back in the bench and crossed his legs. "But you don't have to worry about that one. They are no longer with us."

I didn't know if Benno meant Morales or the informer. I also didn't know if they were still above ground. I decided not to know.

"You need me to come back to P.V.?"

"Eventually." Benno straightened and stood. "I have a piece of work for you. But it can wait, Luke. You need to rest, enjoy the sun, and some good food."

"You think I need rest?"

"I think you look like hell."

I laughed, and Benno joined in. He put his arm on my shoulder and squeezed.

"Hey, Benno, you know a man from around here by the name of Antonio?"

Benno touched his fedora. "I know men of that name, but not from this place. Is he someone I should know?"

"No. Just someone I met."

Benno sat back on the bench and again placed his hand on me.

"Would you like me to arrange a doctor to pay you a visit?"

"Nah. I'm good."

"Indeed you are. Stay here another week. Your bill has already been taken care of. Then I will send a driver for you."

"You know me, Benno. All I need is a decent segunda bus. I like how they take their time. It reminds me never to be in a hurry."

"Fair enough, my friend. I will see you next week."

"What day is it?" I asked.
"Jueves."

That evening, I decided to avoid the noise of the square and instead took a long walk, ending up at a small club. Music flowed onto the street and called me in. I ordered a pair of Pacificos and found a small table next to the band. The lead singer sang a sultry melody while a drummer slid brushes across a snare. A woman in a red lace dress sang a high harmony while a tall man blew soft golden notes into a horn.

Already the events of the last days were starting to wash away. But they wouldn't be gone completely. I'd have nights where I dreamed of guitars being swung at my head, men being shot in the neck, and Nebraska Bob stretched out on a Sayulita street. I wondered where Bob's family was or how long it would be before they found out about his death. The image darkened my mood.

Of course, I'd remember Soleil, or even more so Lucia. I had to trust that they would care for her, and somehow her future would be better than the past. There was no way of knowing what would happen. The violence and darkness that had surrounded her and Lucia's sister still flowed in Sayulita and throughout the country. And if not the two of them, others would succumb to it. But I needed to move away from those dark thoughts before they swallowed me. I had to choose between the high and the low, as Antonio had told me.

Across the small bar, a woman stirring her drink caught my eye. Or I guess we looked at each other at the same time. She smiled, then lifted her margarita to me. I thought about joining her, if only to feel less alone. While I talked myself out of it, she rose from her chair and crossed in front of the band. She held out her hand, I took it, and let myself be led to small square dance area.

The lead singer sang out, "La Luna."

I wasn't much of a dancer, but she was. I let her lead me around as the melody blended with the ocean waves I imagined rolling throughout the night. The horn floated in on a green light from an unknown source. Dancing was a lot like surfing. Or so I thought it must be. The player hit his highest note yet, and I dove in.

THUNDERBOWL

IT WAS TOO DAMN NICE of a day to be pulling a shit job like this—not to mention he had to pick up another jerkwad on the way. Some guy named Smitty. He hated names like that. The sky didn't get any bluer than it was today, not that he thought about shit like that. He left that to the fruity-tooty poets. But this day would grow into the perfect temperature for cracking a cold Miller, sitting out on the deck with a paperback, and watching the odd hawk swoop down and grab a skittering rodent. Instead, he had to lay a pair of boots on someone who'd screwed over his recent boss. He got into the sedan and drove off.

The driver took the ramp off the freeway and eased the black sedan down a nice residential street, the kind where dads talked over the fence and moms drank wine in red plastic mugs. As he drove out of the burby neighborhood, he came onto a narrow street. The houses here didn't have fresh paint jobs, the lawns were half weeds and half brown stuff, and there were no kids on bikes or even a damn wagon. He knew this kind of street. He'd grown up on one.

The driver always skipped breakfast on the day he had a job. His stomach gave a grumble, and he told it to knock it off. He planned on a big breakfast after he finished up, a stack of pancakes and a wall of bacon.

Pulling up to the bungalow with the ugly-ass garage attached, the driver thought about honking. But the hell with it. The guy knew the time as well as he did. When the front door banged open, the one called Smitty came out. He wore a faded plaid shirt and a black pair of jeans over some way-too-white sneakers. What he wore didn't bother the driver as much as what was coming with him. For a second he thought he was bringing along a mop for who knows what reason. When the mop barked, the driver let out a long sigh. The one in plaid opened the passenger door.

"Luther send you? You're a big one," Smitty said.

"What the fuck? This ain't no trip to the vet."

"Yeah, sorry, sorry. My neighbor had to leave in a hurry on the account his wife went to the hospital. He asked me to take care of his dog while he was gone. He's a good boy."

"What? You know what we're doing, right? You're Smitty?"

"Of course I am. But what was I supposed to do?"

"Leave the damn mutt at home and get to business."

"There's no telling when they'd be back. I was told this Luther thing had to happen before noon."

He opened the back door of the sedan and told the mop-dog to get in. A low woof, but no movement.

"C'mon, Larry, get in the back."

He attempted to push the dog's back end and then gave it a boost. The dog protested but loped up onto the seat. Plaid guy got in next to the driver.

"Larry?"

"That's his name. You think I'd make that up?"

"So he's coming with us?"

"He won't be any trouble. He can stay in the car. Let's hit it."

The driver glanced in the rearview mirror, eyeing the hairy beast. A long string of drool dripped from the dog's moustache.

"You ever think one goddamn day about being a professional?"

The driver pulled onto the street and hit a pothole that jarred the whole car. Larry woofed.

"I'm a professional. As much as you are. The mutt won't cause us any trouble, probably will fall asleep. You got what we need?"

"When did you buy those shoes?"

"Yesterday. Nice, right? On sale at the mall and comfy as fuck. Like walking on clouds."

"They're so bright I could read by them," he said. "We get nailed coming out of the place because someone saw your glow-in-the-dark sneakers, I'm gonna bust your head."

"That makes no sense. It's bright as day."

Smitty snatched a pack out of his breast pocket and offered a smoke to the driver. He shook his head, so he flipped one into his mouth and fired it up.

"Crack the window. I don't need your—Jesus Christ, what is that smell?"

"Oh yeah, Larry's been doing that. Something wrong with his digestive tract." Smitty paused. "That's what my neighbor said, anyway."

The driver rolled down his window and pointed a reminder at his passenger to do the same.

"Anyway, whattya got? Pistols, sawed-off, what are we doing?"

The driver signaled and headed down a tree-lined street. The dog barked as a kid rode by on a bike.

"How come only a couple of blocks away from your shithole of a street, there's this nice clean row of houses?"

"My street's not a shithole," Smitty said.

The dog barked again and farted, this time audibly.

The driver swore under his breath, reached down, and flipped on the radio. He took a cassette out of the tray and jammed it in. Soft horns filled in with the brush of drums.

"What's this crap?"

"This is the greatest musician and songwriter that ever lived."

"Doesn't sound like Elvis to me."

It took a lot of internal willpower not to backhand the guy right in the head. He imagined skidding to a stop and kicking his ass to the street. The fucking dog would be next.

"Elvis didn't write songs. He just sang them."

"No shit. You some sort of musicologist? Sounds like something my granny would listen to, and she didn't have any taste for shit."

The driver slammed on the brakes. He turned in his seat and grabbed the guy by his plaid collar. With his other hand he cuffed him hard.

"Hey!"

"Look. I could do this alone. The only reason I'm picking you up is they said they wanted two guys."

"Guy your size could do it alone." Smitty snorted a laugh.

"And they didn't say two guys and a hound that farts like sewer-garbage. So you're gonna shut the hell up, or I'm gonna bust you in the mouth so hard, you'll be eating soup until next fall."

"Okay, okay. Relax. Jesus."

"Burt Bacharach."

"What?"

"That's who this is. Now shut up. And if that beast lets another one rip, he can find his own way home like Lassie did."

"I used to watch that show as a kid."

"Shut up."

Back on the freeway, the driver had to roll his window back up on account of the noise and not wanting a seventy-mile-an-hour wind to blow the hell out of his hair. He wasn't a guy to care about that sort of shit, or worse, skin care. Hell, he knew a guy who had more creams and lotions than his aunty who'd raised him after his dad died and his mom split. Still, he didn't want to go to a job looking like he just came off the tilt-a-whirl.

"Where we going anyway?" Smitty asked.

"Nevada."

"North or South Nevada?"

"North."

The guy was giving him a pain right between the eyebrows.

"Whereabouts?"

"Nevada, near the Parkway. Now shut up. I'm trying to listen to this."

Warwick's voice floated across the car in that angel-way of hers. Underneath was a warm trumpet making soft blats. She was the best for Burt's songs, like he wrote them for her. Maybe he did.

"You really like this crap?"

Before he could stop himself, his fist smashed into the passenger's head. He said *oog*, or something like that. Smitty slumped across the door, his face smooshed on the glass.

"Shit."

Larry muttered from the back. The driver gripped the wheel until his knuckles went white, then as Dionne hit her upper register, he released his grip. A wave of strings floated in the car and brought his anger down. The guy moaned himself awake.

"What the fuck?"

"If you say one more word before we get there, I'm pulling this car over, dragging your ass to the ditch, and putting a bullet in your neck."

"There is no ditch. We're on a freeway."

He grabbed the Glock out of his jacket, his eye still on the road, and pointed it.

"Jesus, okay."

He put the gun away. The tune shifted to that prayer one. He had never told a single soul that this was his morning song—it was a helluva song to wake up to. Who gave a shit if it was about a woman singing about her makeup? The song put him in a good mood, or close enough to one. He slowly moved his head back and forth to the rhythm.

The off-ramp came up, and the driver eased onto it.

"Can I talk?"

"What do you want?"

"Are we going to a house?"

"Don't know. I've just got an address."

"You said Nevada and the Parkway. Where on those streets?"

"It's near there. Have to go down Garden of the Gods."

"What were they smoking when they named these places?"

The sedan weaved through some tree-lined streets. The sun had climbed above the mountains and shot beams at them. The driver turned off the busy road, made a pair of turns, and it was like they were suddenly in a different city.

"It's on this one," the driver said.

The houses thinned out. One had boards on the window, orange tape and stakes on the lawn. A convenience store with a worn sign that read *BLECKERS* had an overflowing trashcan out front.

"This is it."

"The store?"

"No, that."

The driver pointed at a long, low building. The sign in large swooping letters read *THUNDERBOWL*.

"A bowling alley? Are you shitting me?"

"The number on the store is two below the number I have. So that's gotta be it. There's nothing after that."

"You weren't told it was a bowling alley?"

"I didn't ask. Just got the address and the name of the guy."

Past the bowling lanes was an empty lot. Farther ahead, he made out another row of pale houses.

"Maybe it's one of those up there," Smitty said.

"Let's check out the lanes. There's a Browning in the glove box. Take it. It's loaded. Don't shoot your nuts off."

"Funny guy."

The light inside looked as fake as the Colorado sun over the mountains looked real. The walls were painted somewhere between beige and neon yellow, like eggs that had gone off. The crash and clatter was in tandem with mutters, guffaws, and shouts.

"Way to go, Robbie."

"Get out of the gutter."

"Butt crack in lane seven."

The two of them went over to the shoe guy who was using that funky spray stuff, like they all did.

"Have to wait boys. We're all booked up with league play this morning. Maybe come back around three, and I'll fit you in."

"Don't want to bowl."

The shoe guy looked up at the large man in a suit. "Yeah, you look like more of a weightlifter. Whattya press?"

There was a bark outside, which the driver ignored. Smitty grabbed a shoe out of the guy's hand and repeated what his large companion had said.

"Not bowling."

"So I heard. What the fuck do you want then? Food is shitty and the beer is watered down piss."

The driver slid a piece of paper across and pointed a thick finger at it. The guy read the name and looked like he was gonna let a wise-ass comment fly, until he must have seen something in the driver's face. Something that said *fuck with me and you'll be eating your meals with a curly straw.*

"Lanes four and five. They got a semi going on."

"Like a truck?" Smitty asked.

The driver pulled his partner's sleeve, and they headed over to the lanes. There were six of them sharing the two lanes. Their fashion ranged from polyester slacks to chinos, fat collars and bad colors on all of them like they shopped at the same store.

"Which one is Derkins?"

A skinny guy with a long face started to point, and the thick one next to him grabbed his finger.

"Who wants to know?"

The driver rolled his eyes. He had better get pancakes after this shit show.

"I could show you the gun I have under this jacket and say something stupid like *me and my friend called Glock*. But I'd rather just punch you in the head and see how far you can bounce off that plastic chair."

The thick one's eyes widened. He tried to hide the quaver in his jaw, but that never worked. He gave a nod to the guy in checked pants throwing on lane five.

"What's this about?" Skinny asked.

The driver ignored him as the bowler had nailed a strike and was giving one of those arm-elbow-fist jabs. The guy on the lane turned and noticed the large form of the driver looming over his teammates. The team on the other side noticed him too.

"Who are you?" Derkins had his hands on his hips.

"Luther sent us," the driver said.

"Oh, he did. Well big fucking whoop-de-doo. That supposed to scare me?"

"I don't care if it does."

"Who's Luther?" Skinny asked.

"A business associate who is unhappy with a deal we both agreed upon. So he sent Speedledee and Speedledum to pay me a visit," Derkins said.

"Those names are wrong," the driver said.

"What, you're also a fucking librarian?"

"If you have Luther's money, we'll go and leave you to your game."

The three on the other side were sitting back in their seats as far as the plastic would allow. It was someone's turn on the lane, but no one moved.

"Fine."

Derkins threw his hands in the air like he was in an old TV comedy. He walked over to his row of plastic seats and reached below into a bag. The driver glanced back at Smitty and tilted his head. Smitty reached in his jacket, but before he could get the Browning out, Derkins yanked a pistol from the bowling bag and fired. A second before, the driver had pivoted away, and the shot hit Smitty just above his knee, spinning him to the badly carpeted floor.

Five out of six guys shouted *fuck* at the same time, although two might have said *duck*.

The thick one charged the driver and was met by a huge fist to the jaw and a chop to the back of his neck. He bounced off a plastic chair and fell to the floor with a loud smack. Skinny put his hands up in the air.

"What are you doing?" the driver asked.

"Surrendering."

"Fine."

He had his gun out and considered putting a bullet in the joker's neck—except he noticed the other team had run off without their jackets or their balls. They'd followed the stampede of people yelling and pushing their way out the Thunderbowl's narrow doors. The driver also saw that Derkins was gone.

"Shit."

"What the hell, man? Did you know he was packing? I'm going to bleed out." Smitty's voice had moved up a register.

"You'll be fine. Take a jacket and tie it around your leg. Tight."

Thick guy on the carpet groaned, and the driver kicked him in the head.

"Where'd he go?"

"Who?" asked Skinny, still with his hands up.

"Evel Knievel. Who do you think I mean?" He pointed his gun at Skinny's forehead. "Put your stupid hands down."

"Jesus. I don't know."

"You should always keep an eye on your teammate."

The driver fired a bullet into the plastic seat next to Skinny. A large stain appeared on the thin one's pants. Smitty was in the midst of tying the sleeves of a bright yellow jacket on his thigh. The driver scanned the place, surprised at how fast it had emptied out. In his head he calculated how long it would be before the Springs' finest would show up.

"It ain't working. I'm still bleeding."

The driver ignored him. There was movement behind the shoe stand. A can of spray stuff fell over with a clang. He followed the motion with his Glock. Two projectiles came at him too fast to tell the size. One clipped his forehead, and he said *ow*.

A burst of motion, and Derkins was sprinting. He threw another shoe while he ran, but he missed the driver, who just stood and watched. Once Derkins was through the door, the driver followed. Smitty had shouted something, but he'd already stopped listening.

The driver stepped outside and jumped as a metal rod swung at his feet. He tripped and went down hard on one knee, his Glock slipping out of his hand and sliding a few steps away.

Derkins had started to run, still carrying the golf club. There was a popped trunk and a set of clubs spilled out the back onto the asphalt. The bastard must have had one of those auto locks for his trunk. The driver had wanted to buy one of those for years.

Derkins spun around for a last look and saw that the driver was down, bleeding at the knee, with a cut on the forehead.

"Ho-ho, the bigger they fall."

The driver had heard that seven times too many—he decided to make a lesson out of this numbnuts. Luther didn't care what he did with him. He'd told him that.

"*I don't care what you do with him.*"

Luther had a funny voice, low but at the same time kind of squeaky. How the hell did that work? The driver looked up at Derkins holding his Glock and pointing it straight at him. He must have tossed his other shitty piece. Oh, well. Time to check out.

There was a metallic rattle, and a car door opened.

"Thanks for coming, asshole," Derkins said.

A blurry mop was airborne and knocked Derkins to the ground. It was all fur and teeth. Derkins swatted at him, but it was no good. Larry the Wonderdog was in attack mode. He clamped onto Derkins's crotch and shook him until he turned the color of a Sno-Kone before the topping.

The driver retrieved his Glock.

"Larry. Off."

Smitty whistled from the doorway. Larry backed up. Derkins whimpered.

"Call an ambulance. That bastard punctured my balls."

"Let me ask you something," the driver started. "You got any way to pay the debt to Luther?"

"What? I mean, no. Not right now. But I can call someone. I'll get it in a few days."

"Yeah, I'm thinking that's a lie."

The driver fired a shot into his nuts and then one in his forehead. He wasn't an animal. Plus, he didn't want to hear the screams.

"Son of a bitch," Smitty said.

The driver ruffled his hand through the fur on Larry's head.

"Good boy."

He pointed to the still open door, and the dog hopped in the back. Then he tightened the jacket around Smitty's leg and helped him into the front seat.

"Hurts like a fucker."

"First time getting shot?"

"Shit's sake, yes."

"Hmm."

The driver sped out of the lot. He cracked his window, listened for sirens, but still nothing.

"What are we going to do?" Smitty asked.

"Taking you to get patched up."

"Where?"

"Hospital. There's one in Pikes Peak."

"Way the hell up there?"

"It's smaller, they ask less questions."

"Whattya gonna say?" Smitty let out a yelp of pain, and Larry woofed.

"Hunting accident. Mistake at the shooting range. I'll make something up."

"Think they'll buy it?"

"Sure."

The drive was scenic as hell. Even for Colorado it was impressive. He got lucky that there wasn't much traffic. His passenger fell asleep, but he didn't worry about him. The jacket tourniquet was nice and tight. He glanced in the mirror at the cut on his forehead. That would have to fit in his story to the doc. There was a guy named Calder that he'd brought others to see—and one time Doc Calder had to stitch up a nick he got from a wayward knife. He didn't bring the knifer to the hospital on the account that he left the body in the woods.

They triaged Smitty, and it all went as smooth as it could. He went with the hunting story. The bullet had gone clean through, and Smitty hadn't gone into shock. The guy was in better health than he thought.

He took Larry for a long walk down one of the trails. There were a lot of flowers to smell. He stopped along the way to stare at the mountain. Seemed the thing to do. His boots weren't the best for a long walk, but he didn't think about it much. He always liked his boots.

When he came back, they had Smitty all set up in his room. Calder had done a nice job, and the driver slipped him a wad of bills when the nurse's head was turned.

"We'll keep him overnight. Should be fine, but just to make sure," Calder said.

After the doc and nurse exited the small private room, the driver scooched a chair up next to the bed. His large frame barely fit on the small plastic number.

"You'd think a place like this could afford better furniture."

"Where's Larry?"

"In the car. I cracked a window. Bought him a couple of meat sticks."

"You take care of him until I get out of here?"

"What about the neighbors?"

"I lied. Larry's my dog."

"Figures."

The driver looked out the window. The mountain rose up behind a wall of pine trees. It was a nice view, no doubt. The walk had made him hungry, and he wondered where he might get some pancakes.

"Hey. Thanks."

"Sure."

"You gonna tell me your name?" Smitty asked.

"Why?"

"I'd like to know who saved my life."

"I think you would have made it."

"Still."

The driver thought about it.

"I use a lot of names," he said.

"Which one do you use the most?"

"Harold, I guess."

"Thanks Harold."

The driver got up, and the chair squeaked in relief. He exited the hospital and out to the half-full lot. As soon as he got in the car, he scrunched up his face.

"Dammit, Larry. That's the last meat stick you get."

Harold rolled his window down all the way and took in a deep breath of mountain air. He drove off as the sun climbed high above the peak. The sky was still as blue as it gets.

ACKNOWLEDGMENTS

People ask me what I like best about Mexico—they're maybe thinking I'll say the food, the landscape, the ocean, pelicans, or beer. All good things. But the real answer is the people. It might seem kind of odd to thank a whole country of people, but there you go. Whenever I travel to Mexico, I meet some of the most genuine and nicest folks that I've ever come across. For example, this year I met a guy named Antonio. Maybe I'll put him in a book.

Other folks that are on the I-should-really-bake-you-a-cake list are my fantastic editors, Allister Thompson and Rita Lumsden. Each of you provided the most excellent notes and edits that made Luke shine his shiniest. Phil the Art Guy, your cover paintings continue to blow my mind. And to J.D. the layout wizard—you make it all look so damn good. Ray, your insight to Luke's character, and our conversation were invaluable to this book. I hope you know that.

Of course, I need to thank my other readers and encouragers, really too many to mention, but here are a few: Ellie, Dan, Eve, Douglas, Mark, Thomas, Martine, Heather, James, Theresa, Carlotta, Kyle, and Offer. But especially I need to lift a hat, a glass, and a fridge full of cheese sandwiches to my buddy Kenneth M. Gray. You should know you are an engine behind these books lately, one that chugs and pokes along in the best way.

As always, big thanks to my family, all those kids, but not the cats. And a shout out to Jacob, who is the hugest Luke Fischer fan—and to the Lovely, well, for everything else.

Seriously, the next Pacifico is on me.

Craig Terlson
April 2025

Made in United States
North Haven, CT
16 May 2025

68935148R00081